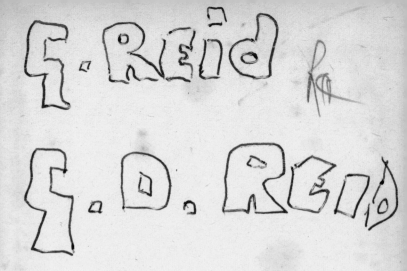

G. Reid

G. D. Reid

WENDI L. SLATER

SEVENTH CAVALRY

by

JEFF JEFFRIES

THE CHILDREN'S PRESS
LONDON AND GLASGOW

This Impression 1971

PRINTED AND MADE IN GREAT BRITAIN

CONTENTS

CHAPTER ONE

UNCLE MOSES HAS NEWS

JIM PETERS was tired out. He had been on the go since shortly before six o'clock that morning, hurrying about the hundred and one chores that his uncle had detailed to him before he left for Julesburg Township in the buggy.

"You'll manage, youngster," Moses Peters had grunted as he stepped up on to the wooden driving seat and reached for the reins. "Hard work never killed a livin' soul—least of all a strappin' young sixteen-year-old like you!"

But that had been many hours ago. Since then Jim had fed the pigs, cleaned out the sties, milked Jenny— their one and only milk cow—and scattered corn for the chickens. He had washed up the breakfast things, cooked a scrappy dinner for himself, and chopped enough kindling wood to keep them supplied for several days. On top of that he had just finished a two hour stint of hoeing in the truck garden behind the cabin— where the tomatoes were ripening fast, and the yellow squashes nestled contentedly in the shade cast by their massive leaves.

"Who'd be a farmer?" he complained bitterly, throwing down the hoe that had become a lead weight in his work-calloused hands. "There are far better things to do than scratch around in the soil for a living. Why, I could be learning to herd cattle, or hunt buffalo, or . . . or . . . fight Indians!"

Still muttering angrily to himself, the boy made his way down between the rows of plants and berry bushes,

5

skirted the sapling shade-tree at the corner of the plot, and came out on the ridge behind the cabin. Here he halted, shading his eyes against the glare of the sun with one brown hand, while he studied the trail which wound up the slope to the homestead from the plain below.

"Not a sign of Uncle Moses," he complained to the open sky, frowning worriedly. "What can have kept him?"

From the ridge the view was superb. In the far distance the late afternoon sun glinted on the lazily moving waters of the South Platte river, which crossed the wide plain of curly brown buffalo grass from west to east. Trees lined its banks in dense clumps, their bushy heads exaggerated by the long shadows cast by the sinking sun.

A tributary of the great Missouri, the South Platte had its source high up in the Rocky Mountains above the mining town of Denver. Fed by the springs and melting winter snows of the great Continental Divide, all of two hundred miles away, it brought its welcome waters to the sun-scorched plains country. There it fed the rich grazing lands and slaked the thirst of a hundred thousand buffalo, wild deer and antelope—besides the rangy, wide-eyed Longhorn steers of the cattle ranchers north of Abilene and Ellsworth.

Following the course of the South Platte, on the higher land to the north of the river, lay the steel tracks of the newly completed Union Pacific railroad which now spanned the continent. It was that same railroad which had brought Jim Peters west a year before. He never looked upon it without remembering the thrill of the thousand-mile journey to join Uncle Moses Peters on his lonely homestead, in what, until recently, had been Indian Territory.

Still frowning, Jim Peters shifted his gaze from the

railroad and examined the sprawling collection of frame-built shacks and stores which made up Julesburg Township. From that distance it was only possible to make out the rough outline of the town. A heat haze shimmered and trembled over it, distorting the details of the buildings, and causing him to blink his eyes with the strain of staring.

"Phew!" he exclaimed aloud. "I'll bet it's stifling hot down there under the tin roofs—or even in that dusty old main street. Perhaps I'm better off up here after all. I can at least get in the shade for a spell if I want to."

He was about to turn away when a slight movement among the trees which hid part of the trail from view caught his eye. Within seconds he spotted a lone horseman move into the open. The horse was plodding slowly up the steep gradient, its head drooping and its feet splayed as though very tired, or suffering badly from the heat of the day. Its rider sat slouched in the saddle, his face hidden, but Jim was able to recognise him by the vivid check of his cotton shirt and the wide-brimmed slouch hat that protected his head and the back of his neck from the burning sun.

"It's Charlie Arcoll!" the boy exclaimed. "I wonder what he's doing on this trail? His place lies over on the other side of the hill."

Even as he spoke his thoughts aloud, Jim Peters sensed the chill of fear at his spine. Had something happened to Uncle Moses? An accident? A hi-jacking in the wild, lawless township? A shooting even?

There was no telling; the unexpected was always happening on the frontier, and in recent months Julesburg had seen more than its share of trouble. Fist fights, six-gun duels and robberies had become common occurrences ever since the tough, swaggering railroad construction gangs had descended upon the plains country.

Jim Peters turned from the ride and broke into a jog-trot down the trail to meet the neighbour who might well be the bearer of bad news.

To the boy's relief, Charlie Arcoll greeted him with his familiar lazy smile.

"Hallo, youngster," he drawled as he drew rein before the panting boy who had appeared at the bend in the trail where the lone cottonwood cast its ample shade.

"Hi, Mr. Arcoll. Have you seen Uncle Moses? He ought to have been back hours ago. I'm worried."

Charlie Arcoll stepped down from the saddle of his dust-caked horse before he answered. Handing the reins to Jim, he sank down on a rock beside the trail and let out a heartfelt sigh. "Man! That's better!" he said, tilting his hat back with a grimy hand, before reaching for a faded handkerchief with which to mop his forehead. "Don't know which one of us is the tiredest—my old hoss or me!"

"Uncle Moses," the boy repeated anxiously, "is he all right? Nothing's happened to him?"

Charlie Arcoll appeared to consider the question carefully for long moments. There was no hurrying him. He had the slow, drawling speech and mannerisms of a man born and bred in the southern states. If he had news to pass on, he would bide his time and tell it in his own way and in his own time. It was infuriating— but it was Charlie Arcoll's way, and there was no altering him.

"Moses was as fit as a flea around noon," he said at length. "But I can't say whether he's still that way."

"What d'you mean, Mr. Arcoll?" Jim queried.

"What I say, son. Your Uncle Moses was a-roarin' an' a-rantin' in Julesburg around noon—just like he always does when he hits the town for a spot of tradin'.

He called Briggs the storekeeper a thievin' rattlesnake for overchargin' him for flour, an' he did likewise with the blacksmith down by the tracks when he charged him a dollar an' a half for checkin' over the wheel rims o' the buggy. In other words, son, your Uncle Moses was enjoyin' himself fine! But he's not in Julesburg now."

Jim Peters was by now completely baffled. "Where is he if he's not in Julesburg?" he demanded, beginning to lose his temper with the farmer's evasive replies.

"Cheyenne," the southerner answered at once. "He hopped aboard the noon freighter out o' Julesburg an' yelled to me to come up here and keep an eye on you 'til he got back."

"*Cheyenne?* But that means he'll be gone for days!"

"Sure does," Charlie Arcoll agreed with a nod of his bony head.

"What on earth has Uncle Moses gone to Cheyenne for?" Jim queried in complete bewilderment.

"Search me," came the drawling reply.

Moses Peters was gone for the best part of five days. During his absence Charlie Arcoll settled himself down to help Jim with the running of the neighbour's homestead as though he had lived there all his life.

Each evening, after the day's work was over, the two of them sat in the cabin and talked until it was time to turn in. Nine times out of ten the conversation turned to life on the frontier since the end of the Civil War.

"I came north and west in '65—after Gettysburg," the lean southerner told the boy on one occasion, with a reminiscent sadness in his voice as he recalled the defeat of the Confederate Army of which he had been a member. "It was still Indian Territory then. The Sioux and the Cheyenne were terrorising the plains. We had to mount guard all day an' all night on the waggon trains, and even then they raided our horse herds an' drove off some o' the stock. I don't mind tellin' you, son, we were right glad when those pesky Injuns were driven back to the Laramie Hills and came to terms with the Army. It was the first time in years that we could sleep sound in our beds without fear o' the red devils creepin' up on us out o' the darkness."

" What are the Sioux like?" Jim Peters asked, his eyes wide with interest as he hung on every word the farmer uttered. The warmth of Charlie Arcoll's reply surprised him when it came.

" The finest horsemen I've ever seen," the lanky southerner told him with grudging admiration. " There's no denyin' it. The Sioux and the Cheyennes are the aristocrats of all the Injuns. An' that Medicine Man o' theirs, old Sitting Bull, is the wiliest son-of-a-gun in the West! You mark my words, youngster. We haven't seen the last o' the Sioux yet by a long chalk. They may be safe on their reservation up in the Dakota Hills at present—but one day they'll break out. Then make sure you've got a good Colt six-shooter at your hip, an' a repeatin' rifle in your saddle bucket. You'll sure enough need both o' them if you're goin' to live to tell the tale."

" Why are you so sure they won't live peacefully up there in the hills for good?" the boy demanded.

" Because they're Injuns," answered Charlie Arcoll with feeling, " an' there's nothin' so all-fired unpredictable, nor yet so proud, as a Sioux Injun."

It was noon on the fifth day when the sound of distant hooves and the rattle of steel-rimmed wheels came to their ears.

" That'll be your Uncle Moses," grunted Charlie Arcoll, pausing from his work of pumping water into the long horse trough that stood in the yard in front of the cabin. " By the sound of it he's in an almighty hurry."

"He always is," grinned Jim, and heard Charlie chuckle his agreement.

Without another word they both stopped work and ambled down to the gateway into the post and rail corral, beyond the hay barn. As they reached it, the hard-driven buggy came in sight on the trail below, and minutes later they were greeting Moses Peters as he hauled on the reins and turned the straining horses in at the gate.

"Whoa there, you long-eared critters! Whoa up I say!" the big man roared, circling the team as they slowed to a halt. "Jim! Tie 'em up—an' don't let 'em get to the water until they've cooled a mite. I don't want hosses o' mine goin' down with colic."

Jim hastened to obey, while his uncle jumped down from the buggy and greeted Charlie Arcoll. He was a tall man, heavily built and inclined to stoutness. He wore his best suit of dark brown broadcloth, heavy boots, and a cotton shirt that had once been white, but was now streaked with dirt and coated with the dust that clung to every garment. A battered Stetson nestled on the back of his head, held under the chin by a thin rawhide thong, and he removed it now to fan his perspiring face—revealing a head of thick jet-black hair which was plentifully streaked with grey.

"Well, Charlie!" he boomed. " I'm mighty obliged to you for watchin' over the boy for me. A man doesn't forget that sort o' kindness in a hurry. You're a good man, Charlie—one o' the best!"

"Jim didn't take much lookin' after," the lean farmer smiled, wincing as Moses Peters clapped him heartily across the back with a hand the size of a plate.

"He's been too busy doin' *your* work for you to get himself into mischief."

Moses Peters put back his head and roared with laughter at the sly dig. "That's what boys are for—eh, Jim?" he guffawed as the three of them made for the cabin and the meal that awaited them.

Jim Peters wasn't amused. Not one word of thanks or praise had his uncle uttered as far as he was concerned. It was all very well to thank Charlie Arcoll—but surely he too was entitled to at least a few compliments for his share in the work over the past five days? "Perhaps I won't always be around to do the dirty work," he muttered sulkily as they entered the cabin.

"Eh? What was that?"

Moses Peters turned to stare at his nephew. "Speak up boy—don't mumble!"

"I said I may not always be here to do your dirty work for you, Uncle!" the boy blazed with a sudden anger which surprised him by its heat. "I'm fed up with this life. It's just work, work, work, from sun-up to sunset!"

Charlie Arcoll turned away at the sudden outburst, busying himself with the pots that bubbled and steamed on the stove. Moses Peters eyed his nephew for a long moment in silence, then sank down into his favourite chair, frowning.

"I didn't know you felt that way, lad," he said with unaccustomed gentleness.

"Forget it, Moses," came Charlie Arcoll's voice from across the room. "The boy's tired out. He's entitled to some praise for the way he has worked since you've been away, and he didn't get it. That's all there is to it."

But Moses Peters shook his head. "No, Charlie," he said slowly. "Jim's right. This sort o' work is only fittin' for those who like it. If your heart's not in it, homesteadin' is a soul-destroyin' occupation. To tell you the truth, that's the way I feel too. That's why I went off to Cheyenne."

"What do you mean, Uncle?" His anger forgotten at the unexpected statement, Jim stared at his uncle in puzzled surprise. Charlie Arcoll turned too, a pot of stew in his right hand, and a wooden spoon poised above it in his left.

"I'm sellin' up," said Moses Peters.

"Selling up?" echoed Charlie Arcoll in amazement. "You're crazy, Moses! This is one o' the best little homesteads hereabouts. Another year or two an' you an' the boy will be set up for life. Given two good seasons you'll be able to engage a hired hand and take things easier."

"Maybe," said Moses Peters, "but my mind's made up, and there's no arguin'. I've got reasons for sellin'— an' good ones at that."

Jim had stood silent since his uncle's startling announcement, his mouth open and an expression of complete bewilderment on his sunburned face. Now he ran his fingers nervously through the lock of straight black hair which was always threatening to cover his left eye, swallowed hard, and found his voice.

"What did you hear in Julesburg, Uncle?" he demanded.

"Plenty. While I was down at the blacksmith's forge a stranger hailed me. He had a letter, written a week ago by an old side-kick o' mine I haven't seen in years. Here it is." Moses Peters reached in his inside pocket and drew out a grubby piece of paper covered in scrawling writing. He handed it to Charlie Arcoll.

"Here, you read it, youngster, you're a better scholar than I am," the tall southerner muttered, handing the paper to Jim after a brief attempt to decipher the smudged handwriting. The boy almost snatched it from his hand, so eager was he to learn what strange message had sent his uncle careering off to Cheyenne at a minute's notice.

"*Dear Moses,*" he read aloud. "*One good turn deserves another and I don't forget the way you staked me when my luck was out in '66. I'm on to something big. Meet me in Cheyenne just as soon as you can make it and I'll let you in on a secret that'll make both our fortunes. I mean it. This is the real McCoy, I promise you.* Signed *Carey Wilson.*"

"That's all there is," said Jim, putting the letter down on the table. "What does it mean, Uncle?"

"An' who's Carey Wilson?" broke in Charlie Arcoll.

A smile lifted the corners of Moses Peters' generous mouth. "The cunningest, craftiest, wickedest old Injun trader I've ever set eyes on," he told them. "He could buy a white buffalo robe from an Injun for the price of a piece o' mirror glass; or a beaver pelt for a string o' beads. He's more of an Injun than Sitting Bull himself when it comes to tradin'! He'll buy anything, an' sell anything—as long as he makes four hundred per cent profit every time!"

"He sounds quite a character," said Charlie Arcoll with a slow smile. "What did he have to tell you when you met him in Cheyenne?"

Moses Peters frowned. "Nothing. By the time I got there he had left the township."

"So you still don't know what the letter was about?" put in Jim with a sigh.

"Oh yes, I do! Wilson left a parcel for me at his hotel. Inside the package was this . . ." Moses Peters drew a buckskin pouch from his pocket, untied the thongs which held the mouth tight shut, and tipped the contents on to the table beside the letter.

Jim found himself regarding a small pile of pieces of mineral rock. He was about to reach for them when Charlie Arcoll dived his hand across the table and lifted a fragment to the light from the open window. "Sufferin' cats!" he exclaimed as he turned the rock over in his palm.

"What is it?" asked the boy impatiently.

"Gold!" answered his uncle with an edge of triumph to his voice. "Take a good look, lad. You'll never see a richer sample o' gold-bearin' rock if you live to be a hundred. Carey Wilson has struck it rich up in the hill country. If I can raise the money to buy a waggon team, an' stores enough to last the winter, I'm headin' north on Wilson's trail just as fast as I can!"

CHAPTER TWO

NIGHT-TRAVELLING STRANGER

" GOLD !"

Jim Peters repeated the exciting word aloud for the
tenth time in as many minutes. His mind was in a
complete whirl. He was oblivious to the earnest argument that was going on between his uncle and Charlie
Arcoll as they helped themselves to food before coming
to join him at the table in the centre of the cabin.

" Gold !" he muttered again. " Gee! That's really
something !"

Already visions of untold wealth and all that it would
mean to them were building up in his mind. He could
picture himself swinging a pick as he hacked the precious yellow metal out of the rocks which had kept their
secret for upwards of two thousand years. He could see
the thoroughbred saddle horses they would buy with
their unexpected fortune; the big house they would
build; the servants they would employ to look after their
every need. He could picture himself walking into
Benson's store in Julesburg and demanding the finest
repeating rifle in the place, and a thousand rounds of
shiny brass cartridges to go with it.

" No more hoeing, nor milking, nor working from
morning to night !" he muttered happily to himself.
" Gee! Won't it be wonderful?"

His uncle's voice, coming abruptly from across the
table, shattered his daydreams in a second.

" Here, lad !" said Moses Peters as he slammed a
heavily-laden platter on to the scarred oaken planks in
front of the boy. " Get yourself outside this little lot,
before Charlie and I eat the whole potful."

16

Obediently Jim reached for the platter, picked up a knife and fork, and began to eat. He hardly tasted the first mouthful, for his mind was still on other, more exciting, things, but with the second mouthful he realised that he was very hungry. It had been a long time since noon, and there was no denying that Charlie was a first-rate cook. He began to wolf the food with silent concentration, and listened while his uncle and the neighbour continued their discussion.

"I still think you're crazy, Moses," the southerner was saying. "This is just a senseless wild-goose chase, if you ask me. What guarantee have you that Carey Wilson is on the level? You've said yourself that he's as cunning as a hyena. How you can think of selling up this place and sinking all your money in a wild-cat gold scheme, I can't imagine! I'd want to know a durned sight more about this strike afore I did the same."

"*I know Carey Wilson!*" repeated Moses Peters. "If he says he's struck it rich, that's good enough for me. And don't try to tell me that sample of ore isn't genuine, Charlie. You know better than that."

"Maybe, Moses," answered Charlie doubtfully. "But all I'm sayin' is that you can count me out. I'd advise you to think again afore you go rushin' into something you might well regret within a couple o' months. Where is this strike? How big is it? How many more people has this Wilson character told about it? I'd want answers to all those questions afore I could be persuaded to sell up and head out into the wilderness after gold."

Moses Peters let out a deep sigh, and shrugged his shoulders resignedly. "Don't ever say I didn't give you the chance, Charlie," he answered. "But if you won't throw in with me, who else can I get to come along? I can't manage a long trek alone, can I?"

Jim's heart missed a beat. "Alone?" he queried,

with sudden fear flooding into his mind. "Alone, Uncle? You won't be alone. You'll have *me* with you to share in the work."

To the boy's horror, Moses Peters snapped at him angrily. "Talk sense, lad, do! You'll have to go back to your aunt in Kansas City. She'll look after you while I'm gone. This is man's work. I can't take a young shaver like you along with me."

It was as though the whole bottom had dropped right out of Jim Peters' world. The thought that he was not included in his uncle's expedition just hadn't occurred to him at all. To get the first taste of high adventure, and then be told that he was too young to take part was more than he could bear. Trembling with rage and humiliation, he pushed his half-eaten food away from him, stumbled to his feet, and stormed out of the cabin without saying another word.

Passing the pump in the gathering darkness, he lashed out at it with his booted foot in an attempt to vent his feelings on some definite object. But it did no good at all, for all he got for his trouble was a badly bruised toe and a shooting pain right up his leg which caused him to cry aloud.

Fighting against the hot tears that were forming fast at the corners of his eyes, he hobbled painfully across the yard to where the horses still stood patiently by the hitching post. Forgotten in the confusion created by Moses Peters' news, they whinnied pleadingly as he approached.

"Gee! I'm sorry, old gal," the boy exclaimed as he hurried forward and felt the velvet soft muzzle of the mare touch his cheek. "I had clean forgotten about you both. You haven't been watered, or rubbed down, or . . . or . . anything."

Bending swiftly under the other horse's nuzzling head, Jim untied the hitch and led the two patient animals to the trough and let them drink their fill, while he rubbed the worst of the caked lather and trail dirt from them.

"I'll have to do the rest in the morning," he told them as he unbuckled their harness and turned them out into the home pasture to graze in the darkness. He leaned against the top rail of the fence for a few moments, listening to the tearing of the sweet young grass as the two horses fed hungrily, pausing every now and then to snuffle and blow down their nostrils, as though expressing their gratitude for being cared for at long last.

Satisfied that all was well, Jim turned away. He was about to hobble back towards the light of the cabin window when he saw the big bulk of his uncle loom out of the darkness before him.

"Good lad!" he heard the big man say. "Seems like you're the only one of us who has any sense or regard for the stock, Jim."

It was only then that Jim Peters realised that he had completely forgotten his anger of quarter of an hour before. So great had been his concern for the welfare of the horses that the scene in the cabin had ceased to fill his thoughts.

"That's all right, Uncle," he said quietly. "I guess you've got a lot on your mind right now."

"That's true enough, lad," agreed his uncle as he put his arm about the boy's shoulders. "But it's no excuse for forgetting to tend the hosses. A man ought to consider his hossflesh before everything else—an' if you ask me you've just proved you're more of a man than I thought you were. If you really want to join me on Carey Wilson's trail, I guess you'll be a big help to me. What d'you say? Will you ride along with your old uncle?"

"*Will I?*" Jim Peters shouted to the night sky. "You bet! When do we start?"

"Just as soon as we can raise the money," his uncle told him with a warm chuckle. "But right now all I'm interested in is a good night's sleep. We've got plenty o' work on our hands from now on—pardner!"

The next few days went by in a flash to Jim Peters. There was so much to do, and so little time to do it in, for his uncle insisted that they must leave the homestead within two weeks at the latest.

Luckily Charlie Arcoll came to the rescue straight away, with an offer of hard-earned cash for the Peters' homestead and the bulk of the tools, in addition to the standing crops. Moses accepted gratefully, delighted at the quickness and convenience of the sale to his friend and neighbour. So pleased was he that he made a present of the house cow and her calf to the lucky southerner, and would have given more if Charlie hadn't stopped him.

"You'll need every penny you can raise if you're aimin' to buy an outfit to last you through a fall and winter," he counselled. "Prices are goin' up every day, Moses. If I were you, I'd put a good few dollars aside —just in case anything goes wrong. Then at least you've got somethin' to fall back on."

But Moses Peters wouldn't hear of it. It was sink or swim as far as he was concerned. He sent word round to the other homesteaders in the Julesburg area, announcing that he was open to offers for his goods and chattels, and for any stock which Charlie Arcoll didn't have the money to buy, or didn't want.

Soon Jim Peters found himself rushed off his feet by the prospective buyers who flocked up the trail to the homestead in search of a bargain. They called at all hours of the day, vying with each other for the pick of the pigs, the chickens, or the household fittings and furniture. They haggled and argued, taking hours to make up their minds, and by the end of the day both Jim

and his uncle were worn out with it all, their throats
parched with all the talking, and their tempers frayed
by the inability of the farmers to make instant decisions.
Like all farmers, the Julesburg homesteaders were determined to make the sale an excuse for a day away from
the drudgery of their own places, and were equally
determined to spin out the welcome holiday for as long
as possible.

But, at last, it was all over. Moses Peters counted
the money, added it to the stack of coins he had received from Charlie Arcoll—and announced that he was
well satisfied.

" Now for our prospectin' outfit!" he chuckled happily to Jim as he made ready for bed, with the bag of
coins tucked safely away under his bunk. " We'll take
a trip into Julesburg to-morrow, sell the buggy and
anything else we're not likely to need, and buy as much
as we can with the proceeds."

By noon on the following morning the Peters' outfit
was complete. There was flour and salt, bacon, coffee
and sugar—all stacked neatly under the light canvas
top of the new waggon. Boxes of shotgun cartridges
rubbed shoulders with neat cartons of rim fire rifle ammunition for the new weapon that Moses Peters had
been unable to resist when he had seen it in Josiah
Briggs' store. There were cooking pots, bed rolls, coils of
rope, and hand tools. A heavy felling axe lay strapped to
the side of the waggon, and steel drums for holding
drinking water were mounted against the backboard in
the shade of the canvas top. Not an inch of space was
wasted, and not one unnecessary item was included—for
Moses Peters was no newcomer to frontier travel and
knew all the snags.

With a flourish of his long freighting whip above the
heads of the team—which had now been increased to
four by the purchase of a pair of matched roans—the

big man urged the horses into action. They crossed the railroad tracks beyond the river and headed for the open prairie.

Their destination was still a secret which had not been divulged to Jim. " It's safer that way, lad," his uncle had said when he pressed for details. But now he couldn't contain his curiosity any longer. Within minutes of leaving the tracks, he demanded to know where the rendezvous with Carey Wilson was.

" Fort Laramie," Moses Peters told him casually, as though it was the next point down the line from Julesburg. " That's his tradin' base—but where the gold lies is *his* secret until we meet up with him."

" *Fort Laramie!*"

Jim Peters was staggered. He had imagined that the old friend of his uncle's was trading somewhere within a hundred miles of Cheyenne. Fort Laramie was way to the north, nestling in the shadows of the Rockies—all of three hundred miles away!

" Why, lad? What's so odd about Laramie?" queried his uncle. " You didn't think Wilson was prospectin' right on our doorstep, did you?"

" I guess I just didn't think at all," said Jim lamely. " I never imagined we were heading up into the Sioux territory. Why! Laramie is where they signed the Treaty with the Army. It's within a hundred miles of the Reservation, and right slap in the middle of the Sioux buffalo grounds."

" Sure," agreed Moses Peters. " But don't let that worry you, lad. The Sioux have been tamed by General Miles, an' General Custer, an' the crack fightin' regiments o' the U.S. Cavalry. There hasn't been a peep outa the Sioux, nor yet the Cheyennes, ever since they were given a reservation all to themselves. Don't worry your head over the Sioux—they're friendly Injuns now."

" I hope so," said Jim Peters thoughtfully, as Charlie Arcoll's words came back to him. " But I'm mighty glad you bought that new rifle, Uncle. I guess I'd better get in a bit of practice between here and Fort Laramie."

Moses Peters put back his head and roared with laughter. " You're too late, lad," he spluttered. " Injun fighting's a thing o' the past. But if you want to try the new rifle you're welcome. Then you can help to keep us supplied with fresh meat when we start minin' with Wilson." He looked across at his nephew, still grinning, and studied his lean, wiry body. " Come to think of it," he added, seriously, after a pause, " It's about time you learned how to handle a six-gun too. There are some pretty tough characters about on the frontier these days, and a man's got to know how to look after himself. Remind me to-night, when we make camp. I'll give you your first lesson."

" Gee, thanks, Uncle!" Jim stammered delightedly, pleased as much by the fact that he had been referred to as a man, as by the prospect of handling his uncle's Colts.

The trail Moses Peters followed out of Julesburg was the famous Platte Trail, carved across the plains by innumerable waggon trains of emigrating settlers over the years.

As trails went, the Platte Trail was as good as any, but it was in no sense a highway. On a good day it was possible to travel as much as thirty miles in the bumping lurching waggon, but an average of twenty miles a day was as much as could be managed on a long run such as the three-hundred-mile stretch between Julesburg and Fort Laramie. After ten days' hard travelling they were still a hundred miles from the Fort and their meeting with Carey Wilson, and they had not encountered a single living soul since leaving Julesburg.

They were camped beneath the stars, only two days' travel from Fort Laramie, when the stranger appeared.

Jim Peters spotted the man first. " Uncle," he called softly to where Moses Peters lay huddled in his blankets, " we've got company."

The big man jerked upright in a second. " Keep him covered with that rifle, lad," he warned, as he reached for his boots and pulled them on hurriedly. " Night-travellin' strangers are poison out on the plains. Inno-cent men keep their ridin' for the daytime." He lum-bered to his feet with surprising agility for a man of his size, snatched up his Colt and slipped it into the waist-band of his trousers.

By now the stranger was in full view, bathed in the pale moonlight as he walked slowly towards them, lead-ing a weary-looking horse by the bridle. Moses Peters moved out on to the trail, his hand on the butt of his revolver. " You're travellin' late, stranger," he remarked in a flat voice, totally devoid of friendliness or humour.

The man looked up with a start, stumbled to a halt, and checked the horse with a gesture. " Glory be to God!" he exclaimed unexpectedly, as he caught sight of the wagon. " Sure an' I thought I was the only livin' soul in this territory—savin' only the prairie dogs, the jackals and the pixies!"

Moses Peters relaxed with a chuckle as the thick Irish brogue poured from the man's lips. " Come an' join us, stranger," he invited with a wave towards the dying embers of the camp fire. " We can offer you a cup o' coffee and a bite to eat. You look as if you can do with both."

" Ye never said a truer word, sorr!" came the reply. " I thank ye kindly for the offer—an' I'm right glad to accept yer hospitality."

As he approached the camp site, Moses Peters stirred the embers of the fire into a blaze, and threw on a few more pieces of wood. The flames flared up to reveal a short, thick-set man in a dark blue jacket of a soldier of the Union Army. He had a round, ruddy-complexioned face, a laughing twinkle in his light blue eyes —and the biggest handlebar moustache that Jim Peters had ever seen. His jacket was the only uniform garment that he wore. His other clothes were a weird assortment of homespun and buckskin, and the hat he sported was a weather-beaten straw affair, without shape or style.

By now Jim had climbed out of his blankets, and stood surveying the man with unmasked curiosity, his rifle slack in his hands.

"What's your name, stranger?" asked Moses Peters.

The ex-soldier drew himself up to his full height, saluted and announced: "Sergeant Patrick O'Keefe, sorr, late of the Michigan Cavalry Brigade—at yer service!"

"Well met, sergeant," grinned Uncle Moses, extending his hand to the man. "My name's Peters, and this is my nephew Jim. Tie your horse an' take the weight off your feet."

"Thank ye kindly. But first I think it my duty to explain how it is a Cavalry man o' my experience comes to be walkin'," the sergeant smiled.

"Please yourself," Moses acknowledged. "The coffee'll take a few minutes to boil."

"Well, it's like this," the stranger continued, settling himself contentedly before the fire. "I was at Laramie when the rumours started. I was all set to ride out to the Black Hills with half a hundred others, but some thievin' spalpeen stole all my kit, and left me with this broken-winded, splay-footed, ornery animal that goes by the name of a horse. Without kit, or money, there was no sense in headin' up into the Badlands, so I was makin' south to try my luck in the cattle country. That long-eared son o' Satan went lame on me fifty miles

out from Laramie. Me only hope was to keep movin'
on foot an' trust in Providence that someone like yerself was camped along the trail. That's the long an'
short of it, sorr, an' I'm right glad I met up with ye
so soon."

Glancing across the fire at his uncle, Jim saw a frown
etched deep across the big man's forehead.

"What's all this about rumours an' ridin' for the
Black Hills?" Moses Peters demanded with a keen
glance at the sergeant. "Rumours of what?"

Patrick O'Keefe looked surprised. "Why! Haven't
ye heard?" he asked. "Some old-timer who trades up
in the Sioux Reservation got himself killed in a brawl
in Fort Laramie a few days ago. When they went to
bury him they found gold ore in his pockets. The boys
put two an' two together—made a dead sure four out o'
the answer—an' hustled for the Black Hills Reservation just as fast as they could."

A sudden silence descended round the camp fire.
The sergeant looked anxiously from Moses to Jim.
"Have I said the wrong thing?" he asked.

Jim Peters answered with another question. "What
was the old-timer's name?" he broke in before his uncle
could speak.

"Wilson. Carey Wilson," said Sergeant Patrick
O'Keefe.

CHAPTER THREE

THE COMING OF THE CAVALRY

FACED by the appalling news that Patrick O'Keefe had just disclosed, Moses Peters slumped dejectedly against the wheel of the waggon and stared at the dancing flames of the fire. Just as the flames were devouring the stout pieces of driftwood and turning them to smoke and ashes, so did the news of Carey Wilson's death and the disclosure of his secret reduce his own plans and ambitions to worse than nothing. He sat without speaking, lost in his own bitter thoughts. It was left to Jim to lift the boiling billy can of coffee from the fire and pour a tin mugful for the sergeant.

Patrick O'Keefe took the mug gratefully, sipping at the scalding liquid with happy sighs of appreciation. "Sure an' there's nothin' like coffee for puttin' new life into a man," he announced. "Take a cup yerself, sorr, an' tell me what this Carey Wilson was to ye."

Moses Peters reached automatically for the billy can and helped himself before passing it back to Jim. Presently he looked up, regarding the Sergeant intently for several seconds before he spoke. "Carey Wilson was awaitin' us in Laramie," he stated bluntly. "We were to share his secret, and help him work his claim. Now that he's dead we've got nothing but a prospectin' out-fit, a little hard cash, an' no idea where the strike was made."

Patrick O'Keefe whistled shrilly through his teeth, plucking at his luxuriant moustache as he thought over Moses Peters' words. Watching him, Jim had an over-powering feeling that their future rested in this stranger's hands. He sensed that Fate had had a hand in their meeting. There was something about the man that inspired confidence and he waited patiently for the ex-Sergeant to speak.

"It's no use cryin' over spilt milk, sorr," he commented at length. "As I see it, there's only one thing to do."

"What's that?" Moses demanded.

"Carry on without your friend Wilson. There's not a doubt about gold being up in the Black Hills for the findin'. I've seen the ore Wilson was carryin' for myself. All that matters is that you get up there as fast as you can, and start diggin' for it before any more folk get the same idea. By-pass Laramie, an' head straight for the Black Hills is my advice."

Moses Peters shrugged. "That's big talk, mister," he said without enthusiasm. "You're forgettin' we don't know the territory. Without some idea o' the terrain, an' the trails, we'd get lost for sure."

"Not if ye had an experienced guide."

A light of interest began to kindle behind Moses Peters' eyes.

"You mean . . .?" he started to say.

"I mean that Sergeant Patrick O'Keefe will be happy to guide ye. Isn't it meself that knows every inch o' that country? Wasn't it the same Patrick O'Keefe who freighted trade goods up into the Black Hills for Carey Wilson himself, not four months ago? If ye're willin', ye've got yourself a pardner, my friend. What d'ye say?"

"Done!" roared Moses Peters, jumping to his feet with his hand outstretched. "Lead me to that gold and half of it's yours!"

"A third," corrected the Irishman with a grin towards Jim.

They hit the foothills of the Black Hills territory three

days later. As yet they had seen no sign of other men, either red or white, but it was evident from the recent tracks in the reddish dust that several outfits were ahead of them.

"Don't worry yer head about them," advised the new guide with the wisdom they were beginning to expect from him. "Concentrate on yer own job, an' forget the others. There hasn't been a gold strike yet that didn't provide enough for a hundred miners. If others strike gold, there's all the more chance of us strikin' it too!"

Tired out and dishevelled from their gruelling journey across country where tracks were non-existent, they still kept going—leaning their shoulders to the wheels of the waggon when they came to the steeper inclines, and jumping aboard on the downhill runs. Moses didn't need the cautionary word from Patrick O'Keefe to watch the condition of the horses. He was well aware that their progress depended more on the four-horse team than on any hardship suffered by the human members of the party. He checked their hooves at every possible opportunity, insisted on careful grooming each night as soon as they had made camp, and generally nursed them as though they were members of the President's escort.

Soon they were high up in the so-called Badlands, with the going getting progressively worse. Everywhere great bluffs of stratified rock erupted towards the haze of cloudless blue sky, like so many chunks of gigantic layer cake. Between these bluffs and crags, deep ravines and gorges split the hillsides as though a crazy man had lashed out with a giant's axe. The heat was intense, beating down upon the travellers' heads continually, drying the sweat upon their brows and withering their bronzed skin to the toughness of buffalo hide.

"What a country!" complained Moses Peters when

they halted beside a stream to water the horses and grab a brief rest from their labours. "It's only fit for Injuns and rattlesnakes!"

"Ye'll find plenty o' both here," grinned Patrick O'Keefe. "The Sioux are watchin' us at this very moment."

"What?" Jim Peters spun around, but though he peered in all directions he couldn't see the slightest sign of human life anywhere. "I can't see anything," he complained. "You're pulling our legs, Pat."

Sergeant O'Keefe chuckled. "Oh no I'm not, son. Didn't ye hear the jackals callin' to one another a while back? That was two braves reportin' our progress to each other. They've had their eyes on us for the past twenty-four hours. From now on we'll have to mount guard at night—or we'll be losin' our hosses to the thievin' varmints."

"Not while I've got a gun in my hands!" roared Moses Peters angrily. "The first red varmint who lays hands on my livestock gets a .45 slug clean through him!"

But Patrick O'Keefe silenced him with a glance. "There'll be no shootin' while I'm leadin' this party," he warned. "If either of ye draw a gun without word from me, I'll quit this party an' leave ye to find yer own way out o' the Black Hills. Let's have that clearly understood, sorr!"

"W-w-what d'you mean?" spluttered Moses, staring in amazement at the ex-soldier. "Are you scared o' Injuns, Patrick?"

Sergeant O'Keefe flushed at the rebuke. "No, sorr!" he blazed with sudden heat. "But 'tis myself that's got sense in his head—which, beggin' yer pardon, sorr, is more than you have! If there's any trouble with the Sioux it'll be our fault—not theirs."

"I don't understand," put in Jim. The Sergeant's

THE COMING OF THE CAVALRY

words were so much double-dutch to him—and, judging by his uncle's blank expression, the same applied to him.

Patrick O'Keefe leaned forward earnestly, emphasising his next words with jabs of his stubby corn cob pipe. "We're trespassin', son," he said seriously. "These are Treaty lands. They belong to the Sioux, an' we have no business to be here. What will happen when we strike gold an' try to stay here—along with hundreds o' other whites—heaven alone knows. That's somethin' we'll have to work out when the time comes. Meanwhile it's up to us to behave ourselves as guests in the redman's territory. If we start throwin' our weight about we'll have ten thousand Sioux down on us in days."

"You mean we're actually *on* the Reservation?" asked Moses in strangely hushed tones.

O'Keefe looked at his new friend in surprise. "Of course we are!" he retorted. "Surely you realise that? We're breakin' the Treaty bein' up here at all. The Sioux have a perfect right to throw us out, an' the U.S. Army should help them do it, by the terms o' the Treaty. But as long as we behave ourselves the Injuns won't bother us. They're tired o' war. All they want is to live at peace on their own lands. It's the 7th Cavalry we've got to be careful of. They're on police duty clear through the Reservation. *It's their job to keep the Sioux in—an' the white men out!*"

"Holy cow!" said Moses Peters. "We sure are stickin' our necks out! I never realised we were breakin' the law by prospectin' up here!"

Patrick O'Keefe got to his feet and knocked out his pipe against the rock he had been sitting on. "That's the position, as plain as the nose on me face, sorr," he stated unconcernedly. "I thought ye realised it—but I was forgettin' ye're both strangers to this territory. Not that it makes any difference," he added with a dare-devil laugh. "I'd stick my neck out a lot further for the chance o' layin' my hands on a fortune!"

"Me too!" laughed Moses Peters as he moved across to the waggon and reached for the bridles of the lead pair.

But Jim Peters was strangely silent. "What's the good of having a Treaty if you break it?" he thought unhappily, and once again Charlie Arcoll's words came back to him as he joined the others, and began to walk up the steep trail again. "*We haven't seen the last o' the Sioux by a long chalk,*" Charlie had said. "*They may be safe on their Reservation at present—but one day they'll break out. There's nothin' so all-fired unpredictable, nor yet so proud, as a Sioux Injun!*"

What better excuse for trouble could there be than trespassing on the Sioux lands by white men who searched greedily for gold? It was enough to make any proud race rise up in anger to protect their legal rights.

With a wisdom far beyond his years Jim Peters knew right then and there that Charlie Arcoll was right. If gold was found in the Black Hills the whole frontier would be ablaze within months!

All through the weeks that followed Jim Peters couldn't get the worrying thoughts out of his mind, and though Patrick O'Keefe and Uncle Moses appeared to brush off the dangers and ignore the fact that they were in the territory illegally, he sensed that they were also none too happy about the position.

By now they had made contact with two other parties of prospectors who were scouring the rugged country for sign of Carey Wilson's original strike. They knew, too, that a further three or four outfits were spaced out beyond the gorge which they had made their centre of operations—on Patrick O'Keefe's advice.

"This is where Wilson was always headin' when he had a spare minute from tradin' with the Sioux," the tough sergeant told them when they first arrived at the gorge. "He tried to make out he was only comin' down here for a spot o' quiet fishin'—but for all the fish he brought back to our camp he might just as well have stayed at home!"

"It's a likely enough place," Moses Peters agreed, as he cast careful glances over the rock formations, and eyed the tumbling waterfall at the far end of the ugly cleft in the towering rocks. "Let's get the pans out an' start right in to sample that bar o' gravel. It's as good a place as any to find the yellow stuff."

"Remember," warned O'Keefe as they unharnessed the horses, and unpacked the prospecting kit. "If the Sioux ride into camp, act real friendly an' find a present for them. Salt an' tobacco are the two things they're short of—but go easy with the supplies; don't be too generous or we'll run out, an' then they may get nasty."

"Presents for heathen Injuns?" protested Moses. "You'll be offerin' them rifles to shoot us with next, Patrick!"

"I'd even do *that*, sorr," laughed the incorrigible sergeant, "if only I thought there was a chance o' diggin' more gold as a result!"

They had been in the gorge three days, without finding a trace of gold in their pans, when the first Indians appeared—two braves and a young boy, each mounted on a scraggy half-wild mustang. They rode down the upper trail into the gorge, halted on a bench of rock above the stream, and watched the white men at work for many minutes, without moving or speaking.

Jim glanced uneasily in their direction, but Patrick

O'Keefe reassured him with a brief word. "Keep
workin', son," he said out of the corner of his mouth.
"Ignore them."

At first Jim thought it impossible to forget the
Indians. All the time he had his back to them he had
an uneasy feeling that at any minute an arrow would
come sailing out across the water—straight for the
middle of his back. But soon he became so engrossed
in watching the sand and gravel being washed out of
his prospecting pan to leave the heavier particles behind, that he did in fact forget all about the silent
witnesses. When he turned around they had disappeared.

From then on they saw quite a lot of the Sioux.
Braves were always popping up out of the shadows of
the rocky cliffs, and staring down at them as though
completely puzzled by the crazy white men who
grubbed about in the shallows, washing endless pans of
sand—which they then proceeded to throw away!

Once or twice a hunter was seen to pass across the
skyline with the carcass of a newly-killed antelope slung
across his back. At other times a whole family of
Indians was seen moving camp on the hillside below
the gorge—the squaw riding behind her lord and
master, with a papoose strapped across her back, and
the tent and camp gear stowed on the sledge-like travois
poles that were dragged behind her pony. But on the
whole the Sioux left the white men strictly alone—
though all the time they knew that they were being
watched.

Moses Peters, Patrick O'Keefe and Jim worked long
hours in their constant search for gold. But after three
weeks they were no nearer finding the slightest trace
than they had been when Moses tried his first pan of
gravel.

It was on the twenty-fourth day that one of the

neighbouring prospectors rode fast down the trail to their camp.

"Trouble!" grunted Patrick O'Keefe.

"Looks like it," agreed Moses. "I wonder what it can be?"

"We'll soon know," came the answer, as they hurried towards the rider.

The man was plainly excited. He flung himself from the saddle and stood panting for breath until they reached him.

"We've just sighted the Cavalry!" he announced. "Two whole troops. They're headed this way!"

Instantly Sergeant O'Keefe took command. "How far away are they?" he demanded curtly.

"Ten miles off, and approachin' fast," the horseman gasped.

"Have they sighted yer camp?"

"I don't reckon so. Not yet," the man told him.

"Right! Ride back to camp an' tell yer boys to pack their gear just as fast as they can an' make for this gorge. We're out o' sight here, an' the troopers'll have to scour the whole country to find us. If I know the Cavalry they'll head straight for the boys on the other side o' the bluffs an' order them out o' the territory."

"Thanks, mister!" the man acknowledged with gratitude. "My pardners will appreciate your help. We'll be right with you!"

Within half an hour the rival prospecting team was safely tucked away in the gorge close to the Peters' outfit, and together the two parties climbed to a high point from which they could watch the approach of the Cavalry.

"Just as I thought," Patrick O'Keefe remarked with a happy sigh as they saw the troopers skirt the bluffs and ride straight on towards the site of the larger collection of white prospectors, beyond the gorge. "All they're concerned with is giving a strong warning to any miners they come across. They won't worry their heads about searchin' out every prospectin' party in the region. As long as we stay quiet up here, they'll not bother us."

But Patrick O'Keefe was wrong. He had barely spoken when one of the men who had climbed higher to watch, through a pair of powerful field glasses, the meeting of the Cavalry with the other prospectors, called down to them.

"They're makin' camp alongside the diggings!" the man cried. "Come up here an' see for yourself, sergeant. I don't understand it."

Patrick O'Keefe sprang forward, scurrying over the rocks with the agility of a mountain goat, and Jim Peters followed hard on his heels. Reaching the man, the sergeant relieved him of the glasses and studied the scene being enacted in the distance with silent concentration.

"I know those faces!" he muttered as he focused on two civilians who were riding with the officers. "They're Government surveyors from Fort Laramie. What in tarnation are they doing up here?"

He hadn't long to wait for the answer, for as he watched he saw the two men dismount and hurry towards the miners, who eyed their approach with unveiled hostility. He saw the officer in charge of the troopers introduce them with a brief gesture. Through the glasses he saw the tension relax from the bearing of the miners, and a smile break over the leader's face. He reached his hand into the pocket of his denims and drew forth a buckskin pouch similar to the one Carey Wilson had sent to Moses Peters.

"What goes on?" Jim Peters demanded impatiently from beside the sergeant. All he could make out from that distance was a vague blur of military and civilian figures.

"Hush, lad," came the answer. "I'm seein' history made right before me very eyes. Those boys have panned gold from that creek—an' they're showin' the Government surveyors where it came from! If this doesn't mean an invasion o' the Black Hills by every two-bit saddle tramp an' drifter within a month I'll eat my hat, an' yours as well!"

Patrick O'Keefe was about to put the field glasses down, when the commanding officer of the troopers swung around, his face coming into full view for the first time.

"No!" exclaimed the sergeant. "It can't be!"

"It can't be what?" demanded Jim.

"The saints be praised!" burbled the hardened old veteran. He snapped the glasses shut and turned towards them with delight written in every line of his face. "'Tis the darlin' man himself!" he chortled happily, his brogue richer and stronger than ever.

"Who?" asked Jim.

"The finest, wildest, bravest officer a man could ever serve under," said Sergeant Patrick O'Keefe with pride. "The darlin' o' the Cavalry—General George Armstrong Custer, himself!"

CHAPTER FOUR

CUSTER

THERE wasn't a man or a boy in America who didn't know the name of Custer almost as well as his own, and living in the plains country as he had for the past months, Jim Peters had heard the great soldier's name repeated time and time again.

"A darlin' man!" was Patrick O'Keefe's expression for General Custer, but there were others who were equally convinced that Custer was the most irresponsible commander in the Army. There was no doubt about it —Custer was either loved or hated. But on one thing all were agreed—the general had risen to the heights as a cavalry commander through sheer dash and valour in the field. He was a brave man, and a striking commander.

Commissioned into the Cavalry from West Point Military Academy before he was twenty-one, Custer had made his mark right from the start. Honours and rewards for gallantry had been showered upon the young officer from Ohio. He was mentioned and promoted in the field so many times that men lost count of his decorations—and even of his rank. At twenty-three he had climbed through the ranks of lieutenant, captain, major, lieutenant-colonel, and colonel, and was brevetted a brigadier-general of the Northern Army of the Civil War. Two years later he rode out to accept the flag of truce from the beaten Confederates—with the rank of major-general—the youngest general ever to be recorded in the United States Army.

With the end of the war, Custer had returned to

peace-time soldiering as commander of the crack 7th
Cavalry Regiment, with the substantive rank of lieutenant-colonel—his previous rank being a temporary,
or acting, brevet rank. But though he was in fact only a
lieutenant-colonel, he was still known and referred to on
the plains as "General" Custer, and he was "The
General" to his loyal, hero-worshipping troopers in the
7th.

"What's Custer doing up here?" the prospectors
puzzled aloud that night as they sat around a smokeless
cooking fire and waited for the fresh killed game to
roast, and the everlasting coffee to boil.

"Search me," grunted Moses Peters. "You'd better
ask Patrick here. He knows more about the Army than
any of us. What's the answer, Patrick?"

The ex-sergeant picked a burning brand out of the
fire, drew deeply on his corn cob pipe, and waited for
it to be well alight before he answered. "Just what I
predicted," he stated modestly. "The news of Carey
Wilson's strike has flashed across America by now. The
Government have heard about it, an' know that folks
like us are scratchin' around in Reservation territory—
where we've no right to be."

"We know all that!" Jim Peters broke in. "What
we want to know, Patrick, is why a man of Custer's
rank should ride in on police duty. He could have sent
a captain or a major on a job like this."

"If ye'll let me have my say, youngster, I'll explain
in me own way an' in me own good time," O'Keefe
reproved the boy with infinite patience. "Put yourself
in the Government's place for a moment. What would
you do if these rumours got to yer ears?"

"I . . . I . . . I guess I'd find out if they were true,"
Jim replied after a little thought.

"Exactly. So what do they do? They telegraph
Custer, as commander of the nearest Army unit, an'

order him to make for the Black Hills with a fast-moving party—as escort to two official surveyors who are experts on gold, and silver, an' every blessed mineral of any value. Follow me?"

"Yes, Patrick, but what I don't see is why it has to be the commander himself?"

Patrick O'Keefe sighed. "Because this is a top secret mission," he explained. "I'll wager a dollar to a bag o' beans that Custer has orders either to report direct to the President of the United States, or to the Secretary for War. The Government aren't silly. They know that if gold *has* been found here there will be almighty trouble with the Sioux. Once they get the surveyors' report via the General, they'll know what to do to prevent bloodshed. That's how I read the situation."

"I guess you're right, Sergeant," agreed the leader of the second prospecting party. "Though how they'll be able to prevent fighting, I'm durned if I can see."

Once again, the army man had an answer. "My bet is they try to buy the land from the Sioux," he stated with conviction.

Moses Peters slapped one ham-like hand into the palm of the other.

"By George, you've hit on it, Patrick!" he bellowed admiringly. "That's a right smart notion."

"There's only one thing wrong with it," grinned the sergeant, as he took his pipe from his mouth and spat accurately at the red hot coals of the fire.

"What's that?"

"The Sioux would never sell. Would you?"

The question remained in Jim Peters' mind for hours afterwards. As he lay in his blankets, well wrapped up against the cold night air of the mountain country, he answered it to his own satisfaction. "Not on your life!" he thought. "If gold was found on *my* land I'd hang on to it like grim death. You wouldn't catch me sellin' up, and watchin' someone else mine it. No fear!"

Daylight came late to the gorge where the two prospecting parties were encamped, for the sun had to climb high above the eastern mountains before its light flooded into the area.

As Jim Peters lay and watched the shafts of sunlight disperse the dense shadows cast by the rocks, he heard a bugle call echo up from the far side of the bluff.

"What does that mean?" he asked Patrick O'Keefe, who was busying himself with the pots and pans as self-appointed cook to the party.

"Breakfast call," came the answer. "Sure an' it does me old heart good to hear it. 'Peas upon a trencher' we named that call when we were servin' our time. You missed Reveille—ye were still asleep, me bucko."

By now the whole camp was astir. The three newcomers to the gorge joined Moses Peters at the creek, where he dashed the ice-cold mountain water against his stubbly cheeks. Jim hurried across and washed beside them, his stomach complaining at being kept so long from the thick slices of farm-cured bacon that were frying appetisingly in Patrick's pans.

"I wish I knew when Custer an' his pesky troopers were goin' to quit the Black Hills," one of the men was saying. "I don't like leavin' that claim of ours without someone to keep an eye on it."

"It'll keep," replied one of his partners sourly. "If you ask me they're welcome to it. We haven't seen a sign o' gold yet—an' we've been up here for weeks now. Those guys over yonder seem to have had all the luck so far."

Patrick O'Keefe got to his feet and stretched lazily. "I'm goin' to have a look at the Army camp," he announced. "Perhaps I can get a clue as to how long they're stayin' up here."

"Can I come too?" Jim put in eagerly.

The sergeant glanced across to where Moses Peters sat. He raised one eyebrow inquiringly. Moses nodded his agreement. "Take good care of him, Patrick," he cautioned. "We don't want either of you gettin' into trouble with the Army—or with the Sioux for that matter."

"'Tis meself that's the soul of discretion," laughed the ex-soldier light-heartedly. "Come along, lad. Here's where you get your first lesson in scoutin' without bein' seen."

An hour later the two of them were high up on the bluff which divided the Peters' camp from the rival prospectors.

Looking back, Jim could see his uncle hard at work down by the creek, washing pan after pan of gravel in his never-ending search for flecks of gold. A little way off the three newcomers were doing the same, as though anxious to give some return in labour for the hospitality they had received since the arrival of the Cavalry.

"Go carefully from now on," Patrick warned as they approached the ridge. "Follow me, an' keep your head down when we reach the skyline."

Obediently Jim crept in Patrick's tracks, and a minute or two later he found himself lying on the brow of the great round-headed bluff, looking down on the Army camp, and the prospectors' diggings.

"Which is Custer?" Jim asked, squinting to try and make out the famous Cavalry commander through the haze of distance.

"The tall one in the buckskin jacket," Patrick informed him. "He refuses to wear regulation dress when he's out on patrol. Just take a look at that slouch hat o' his, too. He designed it himself. He said the regulation Army officer's hat was no use to a fightin' man an' he wouldn't be seen dead in one!"

"Why?" asked Jim, as he took the field glasses Patrick offered to him.

The hero-worshipping ex-sergeant chuckled reminiscently. "He said a soldier needed a hat in which he could fetch water for his horse!"

Jim lined the glasses up as Patrick answered, twiddling the focusing knob gently back and forth. Seconds later the full features of the "General" sprang into view.

Colonel Custer was a fine-looking man—there was no denying it. Tall and lean, and with a thin face burned to a deep mahogany colour by long years of campaigning in varying climates, he looked every inch a soldier. A flowing, fair moustache grew on his top lip, and a mane of golden curls showed plainly below the brim of his campaign hat in approved frontiersman's style. So long was his hair that it nestled on his shoulders, reminding Jim of the pictures of the English Cavaliers he had seen in ancient history books. It was plain to see why the Sioux referred to Custer as "Yellowhair."

Studying the man intently, Jim saw his whole face light up with enthusiasm as he spoke to his companions, illustrating his remarks with extravagant gestures, and the thumping of fist against palm to press home a point.

Jim Peters swung the glasses slightly to see who the General was addressing, and found himself staring at the two civilian surveyors and the leader of the prospectors. In the background a captain and a bugler stood, awaiting orders.

"I wonder what he's saying?" Jim muttered impatiently. Getting no answer he turned to Patrick and found the sergeant was looking in an entirely different direction, as though the camp below no longer interested him.

"Don't move, lad," the Irishman said over his shoulder. "We've got company!"

"Where?"

"Up on the ledge straight ahead of me," came the answer. "The Sioux are just as interested in Custer as we are. There's a party of ten braves an' a sub-chief lining those rocks to the north. Hand me the glasses—quickly."

Jim was about to obey when a bugle blared out from the camp below.

"Assembly," Patrick muttered, still watching the Indians on the ridge.

Jim looked down at the Army camp and saw the troopers hurrying into line, buckling their cartridge belts about them, setting their hats at the correct angle, and dragging their horses forward by their bridles. He heard commands barked out by the officers and the sergeants, and saw the captain step forward to address the massed ranks of blue-uniformed men.

Suddenly a platoon of troopers moved out of line at a brisk command, broke ranks, and ran towards the tents. In what seemed only a matter of seconds to the boy, the white canvas town disappeared, collapsed by the removal of poles and guy ropes. Looking like ants as they scurried about their work, the troopers rolled the tents into neat packs, strapped the poles together, and carried them off to the pack train of mules which awaited their cargoes.

A bugle shrilled again, and General Custer rode out to take his place at the head of the column as the troopers sprang into the saddles of their perfectly-trained horses.

"They're pulling out!" Jim exclaimed.

Patrick O'Keefe put down his field glasses, and

sighed. "They'll be back," he commented grimly. "By the way those Injuns were jabberin' to each other up on the ridge we're goin' to need a whole regiment to keep the peace before winter comes."

CHAPTER FIVE

PARLEY

PATRICK O'KEEFE was right. Within days of Custer's two troops of cavalry leaving the Black Hills, a band of some twenty Sioux bucks—led by a wrinkle-faced medicine man—crossed the skyline, heading straight for the diggings where the soldiers had camped.

"We'd best get across there right away," urged O'Keefe the minute they were sighted. "The boys may need help."

"I guess you're right, Patrick," agreed Moses heavily. "It had to come sooner or later, and I reckon the more strength we can show the better. We'll pick up our three friends on the way over. Come on—let's ride!"

It didn't take many minutes to round up three of the four horses and throw riding saddles across their backs. While Jim pulled hard on the single-cinch strap and buckled the wide leather tight beneath the belly of his mount, Moses Peters crossed to the waggon where the rest of the kit was stored. He returned with his new rifle and the shotgun. "Here, lad," he said quietly. "Take this and fill your pockets with shells—but don't use it unless Patrick gives you the word. Then aim low an' reload as fast as you can."

Mingled emotions filled Jim's mind as he took the shotgun and stepped up into the saddle of the horse: fear, excitement, and pride. He slipped the shotgun into the leather saddle bucket with nervous hands, and watched as Moses Peters unstrapped the gun-belt from around his waist and held it out to Patrick O'Keefe.

46

"You'd best have this," the big man said casually, and the ex-sergeant took it from him with a nod of thanks.

"Let's hope I don't need it," he said as he prepared to mount.

They rode abreast out of the gorge, their horses reined in tightly over the rough rocky trail, but when they reached the open Patrick O'Keefe spurred ahead, leading the way at a gallop for the claim worked by the men who had joined them in the gorge.

They found the miners awaiting them, beside their horses.

"We saw your dust before we spotted the Sioux," the leader grunted briefly. "We've all got weapons o' some sort an' we'll back your play, O'Keefe."

The ex-sergeant nodded, pausing only for the men to mount before he led the whole party hard over the sand and sagebrush for the far side of the bluff.

They reached the third camp as the Sioux began their slow and dignified descent of the final slope. The leader of the miners greeted them warmly.

"My name's Norris—Ted Norris," he announced. "We're right glad to see you fellers. Four of us didn't stand much chance against that ugly-lookin' bunch if they decide to play it rough, but now, with your party alongside us, I guess we're more than a match for them."

"There are ten thousand more where they came from," commented Patrick O'Keefe with dry humour. "This is the time for friendly parley—not fightin', Norris. Warn yer boys to go easy with their guns."

Ted Norris shrugged his wide shoulders. "We'll play it as it comes. If they get ugly we'll blast them off their horses. If all they want is a pow-wow, then that suits us. Spread out, fellers, an' keep your eyes glued on the young bucks—they're the ones to make trouble—not the older ones."

"Keep it friendly—or you'll regret it," repeated the ex-sergeant. "Leave the talkin' to me. I speak the lingo."

Norris shrugged again. "Start talkin', Sergeant," he said sourly as the Indians rode down on to level ground and began to fan out on either side of their medicine man. "But keep it short and sweet. I ain't got much patience with Injuns!"

Jim Peters felt a nudge from his uncle, and turning, saw the big man point to the nearest waggon.

"Ease over there, lad," he ordered. "Keep the bulk o' the wagon between you an' the Sioux, an' don't make a move unless Patrick says so."

Jim did as he was told, strolling unconcernedly towards the waggon, though his heart was pounding fast against his ribs and the palms of his hands were damp where they touched the stock and barrels of his shotgun. He saw the miners taking up their positions around the claim, choosing spots where there was ample cover they could duck behind if trouble started. He leaned against the hot wooden side of the waggon and awaited what was to come.

The Indians came to a halt within fifty yards of the camp and sat their mounts in silence, staring at the scene before them with unveiled hostility in their eyes. They missed nothing. Jim saw them count the horses, examine the waggons, and eye the site of the diggings. They noted the tools that lay about where they had been dropped when the men ran to get their guns, and they paid most attention to the array of firearms held idly in the hands of the grim-faced miners.

The white men too were assessing the strength of their opponents. It reminded Jim of two boxers before a championship fight—looking for weaknesses, and noting points of which to be careful when the fight commenced.

"Pah!" he heard Ted Norris sneer. "They've only got half a dozen rifles between 'em! Order 'em off, Sergeant—or I'll do it for you."

Jim saw him raise his Colt and wave it threateningly at the Sioux.

And then Patrick O'Keefe moved with the grace of a mountain cat.

"Fool!" he spat out, even as his left hand chopped down to send the revolver flying from the man's grasp. "Ye haven't got the sense ye were born with!"

"Why you . . .!"

But Norris never finished his sentence. The Irishman's tight fist slammed upwards with pile-driver force, straight to the miner's chin. He dropped soundlessly to the ground, squirmed once in the dust and then remained where he had fallen—out cold.

"Moses!" the sergeant ordered in a voice that brooked no argument, "watch the spalpeen. If he makes a move 'fore I say so, slam him with your rifle butt." He swung around then, his own gun drawn as he faced the other men who moved protestingly towards him. "Get back, an' stay back!" he rapped out. "The first man who raises his gun has me to reckon with. Take a good look at those Injuns—*there's not a single one wearin' paint!* They're here for a parley, an' by the sainted banks o' Killarney they're goin' to have it."

Without another glance at the miners, the ex-sergeant holstered his gun and stepped out to greet the medicine man with his hand raised shoulder high, palm outward in token of peace.

"What a man!" Jim heard his uncle exclaim. "He's got brains as well as courage."

"You're right enough," one of Norris's men agreed unexpectedly. "Ted always was a fire-eater. He hasn't got any sense when it comes to avoidin' trouble."

A murmur of agreement sounded from all sides as

the men watched Patrick O'Keefe stride out to meet the medicine man who had dismounted, and now stood alone in front of his braves with his hand raised to return the sergeant's greeting.

What followed next proved to everyone in the camp —if they still needed any convincing—that Sergeant Patrick O'Keefe knew more about handling Indians than any manjack amongst them. He knew all the courtesies, he spoke the language, and yet he was firm.

Jim followed every move, fascinated by the whole pantomime that was being played out before him. He saw the sergeant point to the ground in invitation before dropping down to squat cross-legged on the dusty rocks at his feet. The medicine man followed suit, taking his place with great dignity as his braves clustered round.

When the Indian was seated comfortably, the Irish-man reached down to his waist, unbuckled his gunbelt, and laid it aside. The medicine man nodded gravely in silent approval before removing the hunting knife that was his sole weapon and laying that beside the holstered Colt.

Then began the pow-wow. It continued for the best part of an hour, first the red man then the white man having their say. They both jabbered at each other in the tongue-twisting Sioux dialect, aided by sign talk, pictures drawn in the sand at their feet, or by whatever means was available to impress their meaning upon each other.

"I wonder what it's all about," Jim puzzled, as he saw the medicine man point to the hills behind him, and to the sky above.

Moses Peters answered. "He's telling Patrick that these are the lands of the Sioux, and we have no busi-ness here," he grinned. "I wonder what Patrick's answer to that will be? If I know that laughin' Irish-man he'll be spinning such a tale in a minute that the old heathen will be offering to make a present of the whole Reservation to him!"

But when at last the parley came to an end, and the Sioux had departed for their village beyond the hills, Patrick O'Keefe retraced his steps to the camp without a smile on his face.

"I did my best," he announced to the men who gathered to hear his summing up of the conversation. "I smarmed the old devil down, an' gave him our guarantee that we would behave ourselves while we were up in his territory. He said the Sioux had little interest in the yellow metal we seek—they're more concerned over the game we shoot to feed ourselves than they are with the gold we take out of their land."

One of the miners relaxed with a happy sigh. "Then we've got nothing to worry about," he smiled.

Patrick O'Keefe looked round at him with an expression of withering scorn. "I'm glad you think so," he commented sarcastically. "Perhaps you'd like to tell us what we're goin' to live on in the next few weeks. Our rations won't hold out much longer, an' the minute we ride out after fresh meat we can expect trouble. We've had our warnin' to-day. There won't be another, believe you me."

"What else did the medicine man tell you, Patrick?" asked Jim Peters, sensing that the sergeant had more to divulge.

"One other piece of news that I don't like one little bit, Jim. He said his scouts rode in early this morning an' reported twenty wagons heading for the Black Hills. There'll be around sixty gold-hungry prospectors up here by to-morrow night—an' ten times that number when Custer's report leaks out!"

Silence fell on the listening miners as the full meaning of the sergeant's news came to them.

" What d'you suggest we do, Patrick?" asked Moses Peters after a pause.

"One of two things. Either we get out while the goin's good. Or we stay long enough to grab enough gold to make it worth the risk. The decision's up to you, Moses."

Jim looked across at his uncle. Worry lines were etched deep across his forehead and round his eyes as he considered the problem. He took his time before he answered, but when he did there was strength and determination in his voice. " I'm not quittin' 'til I lay my hands on gold, Patrick," he announced. " Not for you, nor the Army, nor the Sioux! We've come a long way, an' we've sunk every dollar we possess in this gamble. With me the gold comes first every time."

"That goes for us too," broke in the leader of the outfit whose claim lay nearest to the gorge. " Frankly, we made our first strike this morning, an' if you ask me there's gold enough here to keep us in luxury for the rest of our days. The Sioux aren't goin' to drive us away from that—whether we're in the right or the wrong about being up here."

"How about your party?" demanded O'Keefe of Ted Norris's partners.

The answer came from behind them, where Norris himself stood listening to the discussion—his presence forgotten until then by all of them. " I'm stayin' here on my claim if I have to drill every gol-durned Injun on the Reservation to do it!" he snarled. " And one thing more, O'Keefe, if you as much as set foot on my claim, so help me, I'll drill you too."

"Now I'm *really* worried," said Sergeant Patrick O'Keefe with a scornful laugh, as he mounted his horse and waited for Moses and Jim to follow suit.

It was a subdued threesome who rode back down the

trail to the gorge. The heat had grown oppressive, as
though Dame Nature had felt that summer was slipping
away too fast, and had gathered the remaining warmth
of the sun for one last defiant gesture before the fall
was upon the land.

" I know what I'm goin' to do," said Jim when they
reached the entrance, and rode in over the rocks beside
the stream, with the hoof beats of their horses drowned
by the cascading waterfall at the far end of the gorge.

" What's that?" asked his uncle.

" I'm goin' swimmin'."

Patrick O'Keefe perked up at the thought. " I'll join
you, lad. Give me a chance to hobble the horses an'
get the saddles off their backs, an' I'll be right with
you. Coming, Moses?"

Moses Peters shook his head. " No, Patrick, not just
now. I've got things on my mind I want to think over
by myself. You go ahead. I'll fix some food."

Stripping quickly, Jim and Patrick O'Keefe raced
each other for the wide pool that opened out beneath
the waterfall, and dived in. The water was so cold it
took their breath away. They reached the surface
panting and gasping for air.

" Mercy on us!" spluttered the Irishman, clutching
at an overhanging shrub for support while he regained
his breath, " I'll not be able to stand much o' this, Jim.
I'm freezed to me marrow already!"

" Me too," grinned the boy. " Let's just race across
the pool, and then get out. Last one across washes the
dishes!"

Neck and neck the boy and the barrel-bodied ex-
sergeant thrashed their way across the pool, striving
with every muscle at their command to avoid the lowly
task of dish washing.

Moses Peters looked up from his labours and ambled
across to see who was to be the winner. " Dead heat!"

he announced with a smile as the two dripping figures staggered up on to the rocks.

"The lad cheated!" Patrick O'Keefe protested with a wink to Moses behind Jim's back.

The boy swung about indignantly. "I did *not*! It was a fair race and you know it!" he cried. "Why! I've a good mind to shove you back in for that, Patrick!" He stepped forward, lunging at the laughing Irishman, tripped over a length of driftwood, and tumbled into the water himself!

Laughing until tears formed in their eyes, Moses and Patrick reached down to help the spluttering boy from the water, but every time they grabbed his arm, one of them would burst into another fit of laughing, and let go. At last, after half a dozen attempts, and half a dozen duckings for Jim, they managed to hold on. Jim found himself being dragged bodily from the water. His toes scraped against the bank. He found a foothold, and thrust hard against it. As he did so, he felt the gravelly bank give way beneath him. He started to yell to his uncle to hold tight, but he was too late. He found himself falling backwards into the water with a splash that echoed through the gorge.

Stung from tip to toe by the impact with the water, Jim struggled to the surface. To his intense surprise he saw his uncle and Patrick O'Keefe dancing on the bank like men possessed of a thousand devils. Arms linked, they pranced and capered and shouted like crazy people.

"*What on earth* . . .?" Jim began to ask as he scrambled up on to the bank, but he never finished the sentence, for there, practically staring him in the face, was the answer to his companions' crazy behaviour. Where the bank had crumbled, three large pebble-like objects gleamed dully up at him.

"Nuggets!" said Jim in a small hushed voice. "Gee! Nuggets of pure gold!"

CHAPTER SIX

THE BUFFALO HUNT

To THE end of his days Jim Peters never forgot the thrill of that moment when he first set eyes on the nuggets. It seemed incredible that after all the long weeks of digging, washing gravel, and searching high and low for even a faint flake of gold in a prospecting pan, they should find the yellow metal they were seeking by sheer accident!

"Gold at the grass roots!" Moses Peters kept repeating to himself in wonder. "I never believed it possible!"

"It's true enough, Moses," grinned Patrick O'Keefe, as he eased one of the nuggets out of the crumbling soil with the blade of his sheath knife and felt the weight of it with a hand that shook with emotion. "I was beginnin' to think we were up here on a fool's errand—but now, by heaven, I feel like you do. It'll take more than a pack o' howlin' Sioux to drive *me* away from the Black Hills!"

"To blazes with the Sioux!" roared Moses, his eyes flashing with triumph. "Quick, Jim. Get hold of a pick an' a couple of shovels. I want to find out how far this strike goes. It may be just a pocket that peters out after a spell."

Jim made for the waggon as fast as his legs would carry him, seized the first tools he could lay his hands on, and returned at the double.

Moses Peters could hardly wait for his return, though Jim was only gone a matter of a few minutes. He snatched the pick from the boy's hands and brought it

down in a vicious jab at the grass and rocks which hid
the precious ore from sight. Patrick caught the shovel
Jim tossed to him, and together, still in their nakedness,
boy and veteran soldier set to work to shovel out the
soil and débris Moses had loosened.

On and on they worked, oblivious to time or tiredness, or the hunger that was already gnawing at their
insides. Jim found himself completely lost to his sur-
roundings, his eyes glued to the widening hole in the
bank of the stream. Every now and again Patrick
pounced forward with a yell of triumph, scrabbling in
the loose dirt to snatch up a promising piece of rock
and add it to the mounting pile beside them.

Panting and puffing like a wounded buffalo, Moses
slashed and jabbed away with his pick, the sweat pouring off him in rivulets, running into his eyes, down his
cheeks, and oozing constantly from every pore in his
body, until his shirt was saturated, and his hair lank
and dark with moisture.

At last the pace began to tell—but not before the
nuggets were becoming few and far between, and it
had become obvious that the bulk of the gold had been
laid bare to their greedy hands.

Moses lowered his pick with a weary sigh, leaned
heavily on the stout ash handle, and gave in. " I'm
dead-beat," he announced—and then, noticing for the
first time the nakedness of his companions, he started
to laugh. " Sufferin' cats!" he bellowed, pointing at
them with a blistered finger. " If you two aren't the
funniest sight I've ever seen!" He collapsed on to a
nearby rock, shaking with uncontrolled laughter which
was caused as much by fatigue and nervous tension as
by the humour of the situation.

Jim turned to look at Patrick, and found the Irishman regarding him with the same incredulous expression that he knew was on his own face. For a second

or two they just stared at each other, noting the dirt and dust and sweat that coated their naked torsos in weird streaks and patterns. Barefoot, and as naked as on the day on which they were born, they looked for all the world like Sioux braves daubed in war paint, or fully prepared for the ordeal of a Sun Dance ceremony.

And then their faces split into wide grins, and they too found themselves laughing uncontrollably, falling upon each other's shoulders, and laughing until the tears ran down their faces, and their muscles cried out in protest at the strain.

"Sure an' I never knew that makin' a fortune could be so funny," the Irishman gurgled weakly as the laughter drained out of him. "Come on, youngster. Let's wash this muck off us—or your uncle will be thinkin' we've joined the Sioux tribe!"

That night Jim Peters slept the sleep of the mentally and physically exhausted. He woke late, aching in every muscle and every bone in his body. He groaned, closed his eyes again, and sank back in his bed.

"What on earth has happened to me?" he asked himself. The thought was no sooner in his head than the magic word "Gold" echoed up from his subconscious mind. He jerked upright, rubbing his eyes for a second or two as the memory of the gold strike they had made the day before came flooding back to him.

Next moment Jim had sprung from his blankets and was watching his uncle and Patrick O'Keefe working away at the claim beside the stream like men possessed. Slipping into his jeans he ran to join them, the aches and pains forgotten in the thrill of further discovery of wealth.

They kept hard at it for days, grudging every minute that they had to leave the diggings for meals or sleep. They suffered disappointment after disappointment when the seam of gold appeared to fade to nothing but bare, valueless rock, and they knew the surge of joy when the ripping of a pickaxe laid bare a further store of gold.

They scarcely noticed the arrival of the new prospectors from Laramie and Fort Remo, so busy were they with their own claim. But eventually they were brought back to reality by the invasion of the gorge that they had long regarded as their own by two well-equipped outfits of hard-faced, uncouth miners.

"Steady, Moses," warned Patrick O'Keefe when Moses Peters exploded with wrath at the invasion. "They're an ugly-lookin' bunch, an' they've got as much right to be here as we have. Take it easy, man. We can't claim the whole territory for ourselves."

Each day saw more and more arrivals. Men came in waggons, on foot, and on broken-down, scraggy horses. They flocked in from all points of the compass—drawn irresistibly to the Black Hills by the release of General Custer's report, and by the wild and exaggerated rumours that were circulating throughout the plains country concerning the richness of the Sioux lands.

All over the west, men were throwing up their jobs, selling their farms and businesses—in just the same way that Moses Peters had—to raise enough money to stake themselves for a winter's prospecting. Soon axes were biting deep into the resinous trunks of pine and spruce trees on the thickly wooded lower slopes which gave the Black Hills their name. Waggons and labouring teams hauled the timber to build cabins, to be sawn into planks for sluices and Long Tom gravel washers, and to build the dams which held the waters of the streams and creeks while the miners searched the beds for gold.

Waking, almost too late, to the fact that if they were to be able to face the bitter winter months, they too would have to build a cabin, Moses and Patrick hurried to the dwindling woods to cut timber for themselves. Grumbling and moaning at the time that was being lost from the claim, they laboured night and day to throw up some semblance of winter quarters—leaving Jim to work the diggings on his own, and discourage any attempt to jump their claim by the unscrupulous riff-raff who were still entering the hills.

So August passed into September, in one monotonous round of heavy, back-breaking labour. The edge of autumn was in the air. Leaves began to take on their vivid colourings, and the grasses of the great buffalo plains to south and west of them ceased growth for yet another season.

Beauty abounded on every side, and in every direction: the beauty of autumnal flowers which clothed the gaunt slopes of sand and rock and shale in thick carpets of bloom; of vivid scarlet of hips and haws on jagged thorned briars; and the multitude of pods and berries in the dense thickets where the jack rabbit and grinning coon shed their summer fur to make way for the downy coats of winter.

There was beauty—and there was ugliness; the man-made ugliness of destruction. Lifeless stumps of what had once been proud, tall trees littered the hillsides, leaving the soil defenceless against wind and rain. Each shower or downpour washed a little more soil away, eroding the banks, draining the land of its fertility. Everywhere the fresh scars of man-made excavations defiled the beauty of the river banks, the creeks, and the hillsides as the sweating, dirt-stained miners tore at the virgin soil of the Sioux Reservation in their search for the elusive paydirt which had blinded them to beauty, ugliness—or even danger.

Danger abounded in the Black Hills that autumn.

The Sioux maintained daily watch upon the comings

and goings of the white invaders. High up among the crags and peaks above the shanty town of rough-hewn buildings that was now known by the name of Deadwood, the feathered braves regarded the scene with mounting anger. Each night they loped back to their lodges with reports of the day's happenings for the medicine men, and the councils of chiefs and sub-chiefs. From village to village the news passed clear across the Reservation. It was learned within hours by word of mouth, or from smoke talk in the still autumn sky by every tribe and sub-tribe of the great Sioux Nation—and by their Cheyenne brothers far out on the buffalo plains.

"The white men speak with forked tongues. They break the Treaty which they swore to honour."

So spoke the messages in the sign talk of the tribes, throughout the length and breadth of the Reservation —one hundred and twenty miles long, sixty miles wide, and covering not far short of sixty thousand square miles in area. They were read by the Ogallala Sioux led by Chiefs Crazy Horse, Low Dog, and Big Road; by the Uncpapa Sioux ruled by Sitting Bull and his sub-chiefs Gall, Crow King, and Black Moon; by the Minneconjous of Chief Hump, the Sans-Arc of Spotted Eagle, and by the Northern Cheyennes of Chiefs Two Moon and White Bull. They were read with anger, and with sadness, and they were interpreted as meaning one thing—war with the white men was inescapable. It needed but one definite action against the security of the tribes to bring the full fury of the proudest of all the Indians down upon the heads of the white miners.

That one move was made, in defiance of Patrick O'Keefe's repeated cautions, by a single miner. His name was Norris—Ted Norris.

The Norris outfit had been the first prospecting party to enter the Black Hills, and so they were the first to eye their dwindling stocks of food and canned goods with growing concern. At first they were content to augment their rations with what small game they could shoot or trap close at hand. Rabbits, hares, and an occasional antelope were easy prey, and the flights of wild duck which settled on the creek in the reddish mauve of sunset were a welcome addition to their larder. With the coming of the new miners in their hundreds the food position became serious. Small game grew increasingly scarce, ducks and geese were already flying south for the winter, and new supplies of flour and dried meat freighted into the mining camp from Fort Laramie rocketed in price as the demand grew.

So it was that Ted Norris and a small party of new-found friends of his own kind threw all caution to the wind. Armed with heavy-calibre Sharp's rifles, and equipped with pack horses in addition to their own mounts, they set off at first light one mid-October morning for the fertile valleys beyond the hills, in search of the buffalo herds they knew dwelt in the interior.

They returned that night, triumphant. Strapped to the indignant pack horses, which snorted nervously at the stench of fresh blood, were the neatly butchered carcasses of two bull buffaloes.

Boasting of their success round the camp fire, where the juicy steaks sizzled and spluttered appetisingly, Ted Norris and his fellow hunters told of a big herd they had discovered ten miles to the north. " Nigh on three hundred head," they estimated. " Just standin' around waitin' to be shot. We're goin' up there again to-morrow with a bigger outfit."

Talk travels fast in a mining camp—faster even than normal on the frontier, where news is scarce at the best of times. When a new day dawned, a score of volunteers rode to join the Norris party in a big-scale hunt.

"Keep your eyes peeled for the Sioux," cautioned one of the older, wiser prospectors as they passed his claim. "If they catch you monkeying with their herds —God help you!"

"What's the matter, Pappy? Scared?" sneered Norris from the saddle of his roan.

The old man shook his head. "No, son," he said. "Just sad to see a young feller like you ridin' out to his death. The Sioux will have your scalp just as sure as God made little apples."

When Jim Peters brought the news of the Norris expedition to his Uncle Moses and Patrick O'Keefe, the sergeant exploded with anger. "I warned that hot-headed fool!" he raved. "Surely he's got the sense to know what he's riskin'? To the plains Indian the buffalo is sacred. You can steal his horse, an' he'll forgive you—but lay one finger on a buffalo he regards as his an' he'll hunt you down an' kill you, if it takes him a year to find the opportunity."

Moses Peters nodded sadly. "That's about the size of it, Patrick," he agreed. Then he turned grave eyes on his nephew. "From now on, Jim, keep close to the claim. Don't ever leave the gorge without Patrick or me—an' make sure there's a gun within reach wherever you are."

"It's as serious as that, is it, Uncle?"

"It couldn't be worse," Moses Peters answered. "I hold no brief for Norris. If he's fool enough to risk his life—well, then that's *his* business. But the Sioux won't look on it that way. They'll blame every white man in the territory. They'll hit hard, and it'll be innocent men who suffer for what Norris and his party do."

It seemed that the same thoughts were passing through the minds of the majority of the miners in the

Deadwood shanty town that day. An ominous quietness pervaded the whole area, from the gorge where the Peters' claim lay, to the distant creek of the Norris outfit. Sensing the atmosphere, Jim Peters found himself pausing in his labours every now and again, his ear cocked to the north for the first sound of gunfire which would announce trouble for the buffalo hunters.

Patrick O'Keefe and Moses Peters worked halfheartedly, for the most part in silence, and when Jim glanced down the gorge to where the new arrivals had staked their claim, he found that two or three of the men had given up work completely. They sat around a cooking fire, drinking coffee—listening.

Hour after hour went by without a suspicion of gunfire from the interior. Morning passed into afternoon, and the tension seemed to ease. Then, suddenly, three single shots drifted back to their ears—to be followed by a fourth and a fifth. Every man in the gorge was on his feet in seconds.

"Buffalo guns!" said Patrick. "They've found the herd!"

"Any minute now," muttered Moses Peters, speaking his thoughts aloud.

He had barely spoken when a crackle of light rifle fire came to their ears—like the muffled sound of a blanket tearing. A chorus of crazy, maniacal yells welled up from the distance. A further burst of firing sounded. Then silence descended on the interior of the Black Hills country; a silence that was shortly to be broken by a renewal of the screaming cries of attacking Sioux and the muffled drumming of horses' hooves over the iron-hard ground.

"They're in a runnin' fight!" Patrick announced. "Let's hope their horses hold out."

To Jim Peters the whole situation had lost all sense. "Can't we help them?" he demanded, horrified by the callousness of the miners, and even his own uncle. "We can't just stand around and listen!"

Moses Peters put one arm about his nephew's shoulders. "There's nothin' we *can* do, lad," he said sorrowfully. "Norris has been warned a dozen times, an' more, but he just wouldn't listen to us. It would be suicide to ride up there—and every man in Deadwood knows it."

"But . . . !" Jim started to say.

"But nothing," Patrick O'Keefe interrupted. "What chance have we got against a thousand Sioux, Jim?"

"*A thousand!*"

"Probably. There may be anything from five hundred to fifteen hundred braves after those boys' hair. Don't forget they've been waitin' for this to happen for weeks. An' this is only the beginnin', lad. The chiefs an' the medicine men have been holdin' the fire-eatin' young bucks in check until now. After the first taste of battle, an' scalpin' an' countin' coup those same bucks will be out o' hand. There'll be no controllin' 'em."

"Gee!"

It was all Jim could find to say as the full extent of the might of the Sioux nation was brought home to him by Patrick's words. Twenty men against a thousand braves; young braves who had come of age during the dull days of peace and had never, until now, known the wild excitement of war, or the lust for blood that turned sane human beings into vicious, merciless savages!

For the second time since he had entered the Black Hills Jim Peters felt the cold finger of fear touch his spine. It was an evil place—of that he was certain— and deep within him he knew that this was the beginning of tragedy and heart-break.

The worst was yet to come.

CHAPTER SEVEN

WAR PARTY!

OF THE twenty men who left Deadwood in the Norris party, only six escaped the vengeance of the Sioux. They burst out of the hills on lathered, wild-eyed horses and spurred down the slopes without pausing until they were safely back among their fellow white men.

"Norris was the first to die," they told the miners who clustered round them and helped them from their exhausted mounts. "He was so durned keen to get among the buffalo he never saw the Sioux. They had us ringed in seconds."

Dazed and shaken, the survivors couldn't stop talking about the massacre they had been so lucky to escape. They told of screaming braves appearing in wave after wave from every side, of the desperate resistance they had put up at first—dropping the massed Indians by the score as they pumped cartridge after cartridge into their rifles, or thumbed shells into six-guns that were almost too hot to handle. They closed their eyes while they recounted the details of the sudden attack, as though trying to shut out the ghastly memory of it all. "If it hadn't been for our horses we would never have made it," they acknowledged gratefully. "There was only one thing to do—pull out, and pull out fast. What happened to the others is anyone's guess. We didn't stay long enough to see."

But though those six men had escaped the first encounter with the redmen, they hadn't seen the last of death and destruction at the hands of the Sioux. That night the braves who had tasted victory struck again, in a fleeting, slashing attack on two of the outlying claims. They rode out of the hills at sunset, killed three defence-less miners, set fire to their cabin, and rode out with a team of captured horses, before a shot could be fired at them by the men who hastened to the aid of their neighbours.

From then on guards were mounted every night, and for a large part of the day. Volunteers took turn and turn about to leave their diggings and take up positions round the camp in constant watch against surprise attacks. Time after time their frenzied shouts and alarm signals hammered out on metal canisters brought the miners streaming to the defence of Deadwood. They grabbed the first weapon they could lay their hands on to beat off the swift-moving braves who darted in to the attack on wiry, sure-footed ponies and half-trained mustangs.

It was a period of strain and tension, and it wasn't long before the weaker of the miners began to crack.

"Ike Walters sold out yesterday and headed for Laramie," Jim Peters told Patrick O'Keefe one morning, when he rode back from the makeshift store that had been erected in the centre of the camp.

Patrick O'Keefe showed little surprise. "He won't be the last," he stated with conviction. "It's only the gold that's keepin' any of us here. If we survive the Sioux attacks, we'll still have a mountain winter to face—an' that'll thin out the weak ones far more than the Injuns will."

But though many of the prospectors packed up as the first bite of winter brought its icy blast to the Black Hills, so did more miners ride into Deadwood—prepared to face all the dangers and hardships of the mining camp in hostile territory for the chance of striking it rich.

"The Cavalry turned us back three times," one old-timer informed Moses Peters when he entered the gorge and staked his claim in the lee of the towering rocks. "They're still policing the approaches an' carryin' out their orders to stop us floodin' into Injun territory. But not even Custer himself can stop a man with the scent of gold in his nostrils from gettin' up here once he's made up his mind."

By now the news of the Norris massacre had reached Fort Laramie. From there it was flashed clear across the frontier and back east to Washington. Immediate offers were made to the Sioux chiefs for the purchase of the part of their lands where gold had been discovered. Envoys rode in to hold parleys with the senior chiefs of the Sioux, and for a few weeks the raids of the hot-headed young braves were halted by the stern counsel of their elders.

The Government tried everything within its powers to persuade the proud Sioux to relinquish their rights to the territory. They offered large sums of ready money. They promised concessions and the extension of hunting rights over larger tracts of the buffalo plains. They showered the Chiefs with presents, and even took Sitting Bull and several of his fellow leaders of the Sioux Nation off to Washington for a sight-seeing trip —in the hope that they would be awed by the strength and wealth of the white men and be intimidated into agreeing to new terms.

All through that bitter winter the parleys and offers continued, and still the Sioux stuck out for their original Treaty rights. Soon the young braves began their sorties again, striking at the miners whenever they felt like it, or when the chance of stealing fresh horses or trade goods presented itself. Small parties, riding against the orders of their own chiefs, slipped out of the Reservation and raided outlying homesteads. Trains were attacked, and stage coaches had to have escorts of troopers from the nearest forts.

Soon public feeling against the Sioux broke into active hatred. The Government itself tired of the negotiations, and looked with alarm upon the increasing raids on innocent settlers and travellers. Orders went out to the Army posts to turn a blind eye to the white miners' encroachment into the Black Hills. The Sioux were now breaking the terms of the Treaty far more than the miners were, and—said the Government—it would need the entire strength of the cavalry and the infantry stationed on the plains to stop gold-hungry miners from sneaking into the territory.

This then was the situation as spring came and the Sioux renewed their savage attacks upon the inhabitants of Deadwood. Officially, peace still reigned, but unofficially everyone knew that frontiersman and redman were in the grips of a deadly contest.

Jim Peters had grown to hate the Black Hills during the long winter that had just passed. Shut up in the makeshift cabin Patrick and his uncle had built in the gorge, he had learned the soul-destroying monotony of life in below-zero weather. Day after day, and week after week the three of them hardly stirred from the cabin for longer than it took to fetch in firewood or fresh snow to melt for water. Time and again they saw their friends die in sudden, senseless attacks. They lived on their nerves for months, with six-guns strapped to their waists at all times, and rifles and shot-guns in constant readiness.

Even Moses Peters had begun to hate Deadwood. "We'll stick it out until the summer—then we'll sell up and beat it for civilisation," he announced unexpectedly one day.

"Suits me," grunted Patrick O'Keefe.

"And me!" grinned Jim. "I'd rather be home-

steading than stuck up here scratching away at dirt and
sand and rock all day."

But the gold held them all in its power. The more
they dug out, or saw appear in the washing pans, the
more they put off thoughts of leaving Deadwood.

So early summer found them still up in the Deadwood area, still mining, still grumbling—and still expecting Indian attacks at any minute of day or night.
It was as though they were tied to the Black Hills by an
invisible thread that could only be broken by some
major upheaval.

It was the Sioux raid in the first week of May that
broke the thread that bound them.

There were only half a dozen young braves in the
raiding party, and three of them were little more than
boys. They had slipped away from their village on the
pretext of going hunting, but once out of the valley,
with the fold in the ground hiding them from the sight
of their elders, they dismounted and tethered the mustangs. Taking medicine bags of doeskin, heavily ornamented with porcupine quills and beads, they gathered
round in a circle and commenced their painting.

First came the streaks of blue-black, ringing their
faces in a broad circle. Then came red and yellow,
smeared thick within the circle—covering cheek bones,
chin and upper lips. Hurriedly they combed out their
long braids, oiling them with sassafras oil, and coiling
them tight about their heads. They took little round
trade mirrors from their pouches and eyed their handi-
work with excited approval, chattering among themselves like forest monkeys about to rob a ground-nut
patch.

Next they checked their weapons, testing the strength
of the new strings they had fitted to their hunting bows,

whetting the blades of their scalping knives against a flat, fine-grained stone.

Only three of them had fire-arms. They were poor weapons, stolen from a trader or taken from a frontier trapper by their fathers in an early raid. One was a smooth-bore musket of which the owner was intensely proud—though his entire stock of ammunition for it had been exhausted many moons before. The other two were ancient rifles, serviceable at close range, but useless at ranges greater than fifty yards.

Their leader was a young man known by the name of He-who-runs-quickly. He was leader by virtue of the single scalp which decorated the horsehair bridle of his war pony. He was the only one among them who had taken part in war, and for this alone he was revered by his companions, and regarded as a mighty warrior.

He-who-runs-quickly waited for the ceremonial painting to be completed. Then he vaulted neatly across his pony and led the eager, glory-seeking youngsters out of the tribal territory, and up into the barren hills.

With the foolishness that comes from a little knowledge, but not enough wisdom, He-who-runs-quickly chose the quietest section of the Deadwood camp for his attack. He knew all about the sentries that were posted round the hills—but he also knew that as the heat of day mounted the sentries grew careless and had been seen to doze over their rifles.

What He-who-runs-quickly didn't know was that the section he had chosen to attack was the gorge where the Peters' claim lay—nor did he know that the sentry on duty high above was an Army man, trained by long years of harsh discipline to keep his eyes and his wits about him at all times, with barely a flicker of an eyelid to denote his tiredness.

The sentry was Patrick O'Keefe.

Patrick spotted the raiders the minute they crossed

the skyline. As He-who-runs-quickly mounted the crest, and paused to select the path his war party was to follow to the gorge, the ex-sergeant already had him full in the sights of his rifle.

Patrick only waited long enough to identify the leader. He noted the war paint, and saw the raw-boned youths who followed close behind. Then, selecting the very spot that was to be his target, the Irishman followed the young brave into the descent, swinging his rifle expertly to keep pace with him—and squeezed the trigger.

He-who-runs-quickly never heard the shot, nor knew what hit him. He crumpled sideways and fell from his pony's back—oblivious to the startled cries of his companions, and of the stentorian warning cry that rose up from Patrick O'Keefe's lips and echoed up and down the gorge.

Working by the stream, Jim and Moses Peters heard the cries. They flung aside their tools, snatched up their guns, and were just in time to see Patrick silhouetted against the sky, pumping shot after well-aimed shot into the would-be warriors.

"Hold your fire, lad," warned Moses as Jim levelled his rifle and prepared to blaze at the jumbled mass of horses and feathered, painted riders. "They'll break this way. They can't go back or Patrick will down them. Get behind the cabin, and make every shot tell when they reach the stream. Aim at the hosses!"

Taking to his heels, Jim Peters ran hard for the cabin, flung himself round the corner of the rough-hewn building, and trained his rifle on the spot where the braves would have to cross if they were to escape. He saw his uncle drop down behind the wooden sluice, clutching the shot-gun, and with his Colt laid ready by his side.

Panic-stricken by the loss of their leader, and by the

merciless fire that was ripping into them from above, the Sioux youths dug their heels hard into the sides of their mounts and raced for the floor of the gorge.

On and on they came, careering down the slope in a shower of loose rock and dust. They saw the miners at the far end of the gorge fling themselves flat and open fire from behind the boulders that littered the gorge. With terror in their eyes they took the only chance. They raced madly down the gorge, straight for the waiting miners, their heads low to the necks of their ponies as they yelled their crazy war-cries.

Jim Peters, obeying his uncle's instructions to the letter, held himself in check until the Indians reached the stream bank. Then he sighted quickly, and pressed the trigger. The leading pony turned a sudden somersault and hurled its rider into the water.

What happened next was just a confused memory. Dust rolled high in all directions, the noise was deafening, and it was impossible to identify the shouts of the defenders from the war cries of the attackers. All Jim remembered was the continual crash of exploding guns, the smell of powder, and the jumping of his rifle butt against his shoulder as he fired, re-loaded, and fired again.

In seconds the battle was over. The war party that He-who-runs-quickly had intended should bring back white men's scalps and trophies to prove their manhood, lay utterly destroyed. Four riderless horses pranced around the gorge, and two more lay dead in their tracks.

Jim staggered to his feet, shaken, but exultant that he had acquitted himself with calm efficiency at the testing time that he had dreaded. He moved out from the cabin, and saw Patrick O'Keefe running down the hillside towards him.

"All right, lad?" the Irishman shouted as he caught sight of him.

"I guess so," Jim heard himself answer.

"Where's yer uncle?"

It was only then that Jim realised he hadn't seen his uncle since he had dropped down beside the sluice. "I don't know," he yelled back. "He was over there when it started."

Still dazed, and with the thunder of gunfire still ringing in his ears, Jim saw Patrick follow the line of his pointing finger and hasten to the bank.

By now the other miners had caught the horses, and were crowding up the gorge to join them.

"Crazy young bucks," one of the men was saying. "They never stood a chance. O'Keefe had 'em pinned from the moment they showed their noses."

"Not a mite o' damage, an' no one hurt," grinned a second man happily to Jim. "You did well, youngster."

But Jim hardly heard him. He was watching Patrick O'Keefe.

The Irishman was bending over the shadows beside the heavy wooden sluice. There was something in the way he stood that brought a sudden fear to the boy. He started to run forward, but the sergeant's voice halted him.

"Stay where ye are, lad," the Irishman said softly across the settling dust of the stifling gorge. "Yer uncle's been hurt."

Jim moved forward, to be stopped by a brawny arm. "Best not to see, son," said a stranger's voice. "Death ain't pleasant for a youngster to look upon."

CHAPTER EIGHT

SURPRISE FOR THE ADJUTANT

For days Jim Peters was so shocked and stunned by the death of his uncle that he could not accept that it was true. He kept expecting the big man to appear round the bend in the gorge, and to hear again his deep-throated laugh. Every time he heard the ring of a pick-axe against solid rock, he looked up from the cabin where he sat and brooded—but it was always someone else who wielded the pick, never the kindly, obstinate man who had been his only living male relative.

For a while Patrick O'Keefe and the other miners left Jim alone to nurse his grief, but after two days the unsmiling Irishman tried to jerk him out of his misery and take a hand with the daily routine of the claim.

"It's hard, lad," he said gently, "but life has to go on. Moses would have wanted it that way."

"We should never have come here!" Jim blazed in sudden anger. "It's been nothing but trouble and worry from the moment we set foot in the Black Hills. Why did Uncle Moses have to die, Patrick? What had he ever done to hurt the Sioux? He was a good man. All he wanted was the chance to dig enough gold to keep us both in comfort."

"Ye've put your finger on it there," said Patrick O'Keefe as he puffed at his corn-cob pipe. "It's the gold, lad. It gets under yer hide somehow, an' you just have to go on gettin' more an' more an' more. There's no sense in it—but ye can't help yerself. If ye ask me, Jim, there are things that are a sight more important than gold, or money."

" Such as?"

" Such as doin' what ye want to do with yer life, an' not bein' a slave to the yellow stuff. Take me, for example. I've never been really happy since I left the Army. It was a man's life, an' it was a job I understood —hard work, companionship, an' the knowledge that ye were doin' somethin' worth while."

" Killing!" said Jim with bitterness.

Patrick O'Keefe rounded on him angrily. " No son!" he exploded. " There's nothin' pleasant about killin'. That's what we have an Army for—*to stop people killin' each other*. Men like Custer, an' General Miles an' General Terry fought to *save* life. They used their brains an' their strength to protect the settlers whose only wish was to farm in peace. They subdued the Apaches, an' slammed the Comanches, an' drove the Sioux into makin' peace."

" Peace!" Jim Peters sneered the word. " Do you call this peace, Patrick? Did Uncle Moses die peacefully? Have we got peace up here in the Black Hills when the filthy savages can ride in an' kill an innocent man for no reason at all?"

Patrick O'Keefe took the pipe from his mouth and looked levelly at the bitter, angry boy. " Think, lad," he suggested quietly. " Who made the first move up here? Whose lands are these? Tell me that an' ye'll realise that we're all to blame—not just the Sioux. Yer uncle knew the risk he was takin' when he rode in after gold. Ye knew it an' so did I. There was peace until we came here—peace that was brought about by the work o' the Army."

" . . . and now we've undone all their work by our greed for gold," said Jim as the truth came to him with sudden, brilliant clarity.

Patrick O'Keefe rose to his feet and knocked out his pipe. " That's about the size of it, Jim," he said. " The only hope for this territory is an Army strong enough to keep the Sioux subdued—an' the white men under control. If there had been enough soldiers stationed up here not a single miner would have got into the Black Hills, and' there wouldn't have been any o' this heartache an' bloodshed."

Jim Peters was silent for a long time as he digested Patrick's words. "Why aren't there enough soldiers?" he asked at length.

Patrick sighed. "Because there are easier ways o' makin' a livin'. We're makin' more in a day on this claim than a captain makes in a month. The Army just can't get enough volunteers."

"I see."

Jim thought about Patrick's words all through the remainder of the day. For the first time since the Indian attack his mind was occupied by thoughts other than of the death of his uncle, and his grief had been crowded to the back of his mind.

That night, as they prepared their evening meal and saw the guards take up their positions around the hills, Jim's thoughts forsook the past and the present, and looked instead at the future that lay before him. What did he want out of life? What were his aims and ambitions?

"I don't want to stay up here an' dig gold," he announced aloud with a suddenness that made Patrick O'Keefe jump.

"What *do* ye want to do, lad?" the sergeant demanded. "I guess it's my job to advise ye now, an' I'll be right glad to help ye make up your mind, an' go along with ye. Reckon yer welfare is my responsibility now Moses has gone."

Jim Peters regarded the burly, moustached Irishman across the camp fire. For the first time he saw the worry that had eaten deep into his friend's face in the past few days. He read the gentle kindness that Patrick tried to hide behind his stern, disciplined bearing, and the sadness he was suffering at the loss of Moses Peters. Jim had hardly realised how much a part of their lives the ex-soldier had become since they met him out on the Platte Trail. Affection welled up within him.

"Will you come with me, Patrick?" he blurted out.

"Anywhere ye say, lad," the Irishman told him with simple honesty. "What have ye got in mind?"

"I want to join the Army if they'll have me."

Once he had made the decision, Jim knew that it was right. There was no shifting him—he had inherited the Peters' obstinacy. Secretly Patrick O'Keefe was delighted. His heart warmed to the youngster, but he put up every objection he could think of to see if he could put Jim off. "Ye're too young," he began. Jim laughed. "Too young my foot!" he exclaimed. "I'll soon be seventeen, and I look older. I know how to use a rifle and a revolver. I can ride, and I'm as tough as nails."

"It's too dangerous," Patrick protested. "There's goin' to be big trouble with the Sioux."

"It couldn't be more dangerous than staying up here," Jim stated bitterly. "It's no good arguing, Patrick. My mind's made up. From what you've told me the Army wants volunteers, and they'll take me if I can convince them I'm old enough and strong enough. That shouldn't be hard."

But still Patrick O'Keefe shook his head. "They'll not take ye in the ranks, Jim," he said firmly. "Eighteen's the lowest age. Yer only chance is to volunteer as a bugler."

Jim shrugged his shoulders. "All right. I'll go as a bugler. I don't care what I do as long as I get in the Army."

" The Cavalry," Patrick corrected him with a sudden grin. " The Seventh Cavalry is the place for both o' us. We'll go an' see Custer himself!"

Jim and Patrick O'Keefe lost no time in leaving Deadwood and the Black Hills territory. They sold out their claim to the neighbours for a good price, bartered the waggon and most of their kit for stores and pack saddles, and banked their money at the first reasonably large settlement that they struck.

" We'll leave it there as a nice little nest egg," Patrick smiled. " Money's no good to ye in the Army, Jim, but it's mighty useful when ye come out after servin' yer time."

" Is it safe?" Jim asked, for this was his first experience of handling more than a few dollars.

" Sure an' 'tis safe as the White House at Washington," Patrick told him. " What's more it will earn interest for us all the time we leave it there."

" Now where do we head?" the boy asked, once the worry of their finances had dissolved. " Fort Laramie?"

" No. Bismark. That's way up north on the Missouri. Fort Abraham Lincoln lies across the river, an' that's where we'll find the headquarters o' the Seventh."

" You're the boss, Sergeant," smiled Jim. " Let's ride."

It was well into June before they reached Bismark. Taking rooms for the night in a busy hotel, they rose early and caught the ferry across the river.

The Missouri was wide, and the crossing they made was slow. It gave them ample opportunity to study the fort and see the full extent of the Cavalry headquarters. It was far bigger than Jim had imagined.

Fort Abraham Lincoln had not been built long. It was one of the latest of the forts placed at strategic places throughout the plains country. Not only was it the base for Custer's famous regiment, but it was also an important supply depot, with a stout jetty and unloading piers for the steamboats which nosed up the Missouri with provisions, ammunition, and stores for men and horses. Long, low, single-storied barracks buildings stood in neat rows, one after another round the hard-panned parade ground. Lines and lines of stables and wash-houses interspersed them, and to one side were the officers' married quarters, and the frame-built houses where the wives and families of the sergeants and other ranks lived.

Stepping from the ferry, Jim and Patrick passed under the archway that stretched across the main gate and bore the regimental insignia of the Seventh Cavalry —crossed sabres, with the " 7th " in their shadow. A sentry stopped them at once.

" Who d'you wish to see?" he demanded.

" General Custer," Patrick told him.

The sentry laughed. " You can't just walk in an' see the General," he said with scorn. " Who d'you think you are—the President?"

Patrick O'Keefe flushed, and Jim was hard put to suppress the grin that threatened to break across his lips.

" Young man," said Patrick icily, " I was a soldier before ye were out o' yer cradle, an' 'tis myself that knows who I can see or who I cannot see. I've come three hundred miles to speak with the General, an' I'll not be put off by any lip from a young whippersnapper like yerself."

It was the sentry's turn to blush. " What's your business?" he asked angrily.

" That's between the General an' myself," Patrick stated with a trace of pomposity as he stared back at the self-important young soldier. " Hurry man! We haven't got all day to waste. Take me to the General's quarters or show me where the Adjutant's office lies, or I'll not be answerable for what happens to ye when the General hears how ye've held me up at the gate o' this Fort."

There was something in the tone of Patrick's voice which made the sentry realise he was not dealing with just another civilian. He hesitated no more. "Follow me," he said, shouting to the guardhouse for a relief to take over in his absence.

"You were a bit hard on him, weren't you, Patrick?" Jim whispered as they crossed the parade ground and made for the Adjutant's office.

Patrick O'Keefe grinned. "No, lad—not hard. It's just that the minute I get the smell o' Army posts an' cavalry stables in me nostrils I start imaginin' I'm back with three stripes on me sleeve, and I won't take impertinence from anyone. Besides, I once saw an Army scout held up at the gate by a cocky young sentry when he had an urgent report for the commander. If ye had heard the commander's language an hour later ye wouldn't have forgotten either!"

"Who was the commander?" Jim asked as they approached the raised walk before the painted door with ADJUTANT written in large white letters across its panels.

"Custer!" smiled Patrick reminiscently. "An' I was the sentry!"

Lt. Cooke looked up from his plain deal desk and eyed the new arrivals critically.

Jim Peters stood stiffly beside Patrick O'Keefe, and sucked in his cheeks in an attempt to make himself look older and more manly than he was, or felt. He could almost feel the Adjutant's eyes boring into him, so intently did they stare at his rough, travel-stained clothing, and the heavy iron-tipped boots which had

been so serviceable up in the Black Hills, but now felt
awkward and clumsy in the boarded office.

"What can I do for you?" asked the first lieutenant
when he had completed his careful scrutiny, and dis-
missed the sentry.

"I wish to speak with General Custer," Patrick
repeated.

The adjutant frowned. "*Lieutenant-Colonel* Custer,"
he said sourly.

"Beggin' your pardon, sorr," said Patrick. "I was
forgettin'. I served under the Lieutenant-Colonel when
he was my General."

Lt. Cooke sat back in his chair and raised one eyebrow.

"Regiment?" he demanded.

"Michigan Cavalry Brigade—Union Army. Rank o'
sergeant, sorr."

Lieutenant Cooke successfully raised the other eyebrow. "Where are you from now?"

"The Black Hills, sorr."

Lieutenant Cooke's chair crashed back on to the
board floor with a sudden jerk. "Are you, by George!"
he exclaimed. "Colonel Custer *will* be pleased to see
you, sergeant! Come with me."

CHAPTER NINE

LIEUTENANT-COLONEL George Armstrong Custer sat on the edge of his desk with both legs dangling into space. His large, capable right hand was folded round the hilt of a bared sabre, with which he chopped the air while he listened to Patrick O'Keefe's outline of the existing conditions up in the Black Hills.

Jim Peters had sat stock still on the very edge of a hard wooden chair—completely overawed by the presence of the famed commander of the Seventh Cavalry. Five minutes before, a nagging tickle had developed in his throat, but he didn't dare to cough for fear of interrupting Patrick's flow of words—nor did he wish to distract the Colonel. He just kept swallowing, and hoping for the best.

"That's very interesting, O'Keefe," said the commander when Patrick came to the end of his description of the attack in which Moses Peters had died. "I've had precious little up-to-date, eye-witness accounts of the conditions up in Deadwood. Your report is very valuable to me."

"Thank ye, sorr," smiled the Irishman. "I thought ye would like to hear it from me own lips. Ye trained me to report the slightest thing I saw when ye were me company commander in the War."

A chuckle broke from the Colonel's lips. "Still the same old Irish blarney, Sergeant," he laughed. "You haven't altered, O'Keefe."

"No sorr," Patrick agreed, a little doubtfully, for he wasn't quite sure what Custer was getting at.

"Do you think I'm silly enough to think you came all the way up to Bismark from Deadwood just to let me know what my scouts are reporting every week?" the Colonel inquired with a twinkle in his shrewd blue eyes. "I'm ashamed of you, Sergeant—you ought to know me better than that."

"Well, sorr," Patrick blustered, searching hurriedly for words with which to hide his confusion now that Custer had seen through his carefully thought out ruse. "I . . . I . . ."

"You wanted to ask me a favour, and you thought the best way to do it was to make me a present of some useful information. Is that what you were going to say?"

Patrick O'Keefe had the grace to colour up for the second time that day. "To tell the truth, sorr—yes!" he grinned.

"I thought so! Out with it, Sergeant. What is it you want?"

"To re-enlist, sorr, an' serve under yer command again," Patrick O'Keefe requested earnestly.

Lieutenant-Colonel Custer smiled. "That shouldn't be difficult, O'Keefe," he said, still swinging his sabre through the air in intricate patterns. "You served me well before, and I see no reason why you shouldn't serve the 7th just as well. Permission granted—subject to medical examination. I'll inform the Adjutant to swear you in to-morrow."

"Thank ye, sorr," said Patrick gratefully. He paused, twirling his moustache nervously. "There's just one other thing, General," he added.

"Out with it."

"The lad here. He wants to join up too."

The Colonel's sabre checked in mid-air. Jim saw the gleaming point swing around until it was aimed straight at him, within a few inches of his nose.

"On your feet, lad," Patrick said in a hoarse stage whisper that brought Jim to his feet in a second, his boots thudding to the floor, and his thin body held rigidly at attention, chin up, eyes straight ahead.

The sabre point came up and began to swish to and fro beneath his nose as the Colonel looked him over as though he was examining a horse to assess its capabilities. Jim didn't move as much as an eyelash.

"How old are you, boy?" came the question he had been dreading.

"Eighteen, sir," Jim told him in a husky voice.

"You're a liar!" roared Custer.

"Yes, sir," said Jim unhappily.

"How old *are* you?"

"Crowding seventeen, sir."

"Hmmph!"

A dreadful silence descended upon the room, and Jim found himself holding his breath, not daring to breathe as the Colonel slid to his feet and walked around him with slow, deliberate strides of his spurred cavalry boots. He felt the claw-like grip of Custer's bony fingers on his biceps, and heard the non-committal grunt.

"Can you ride?"

"Yessir. Saddled or bareback, sir. And I can drive a team, sir."

"Hmmph! Can you fight?"

Patrick answered for him. "He was as cool as a cucumber when the Sioux struck, sorr. He dropped the lead horse with his first shot."

"Did he?" said Custer with interest, and Jim began to gain hope.

"Rifle, revolver or shot-gun, sir," he broke in. "I can use them all. My uncle trained me on the way to the Black Hills."

"Can you blow a bugle?"

"No, sir," Jim admitted, and his hopes began to fade again.

"Neither can I!" chuckled Custer. "Report to the Adjutant in the morning. He'll swear you in *if you tell him you're eighteen.* Understand?"

"Yessir!" grinned Jim. "Thank you, sir!"

Within five minutes of raising his right hand to swear the oath of allegiance, Jim Peters found himself alone in a strange, harsh man's world. Somehow he had presumed that Patrick O'Keefe would always be at his side to guide him through the first uncertain days of Army life, but it hadn't turned out that way. Patrick O'Keefe had re-enlisted as a private, his previous rank being noted but carrying no weight in the new regiment. Not only that, but the Irishman who had become Jim's friend and guide and adviser had been posted to " C " company, while he himself had been swallowed up in the ranks of " I " company.

"When do I see you, Patrick?" Jim asked with sudden panic.

"Ye don't, lad. Ye're on yer own from now on—it's the only way. Learn as fast as ye can, do what ye're told without question, an' keep yer nose clean. If ye come runnin' to me every five minutes ye'll be a marked man in yer company. There isn't a soldier born who likes or respects a man who can't take care o' himself."

"You mean I'll *never* be allowed to be with you?" Jim asked unhappily.

"Not until ye're trained an' accepted as a member o' the regiment," Patrick told him firmly. "Rookies an' veterans don't mix, lad."

"Oh," said Jim, "I see."

"It's not quite as bad as that," Patrick put in hurriedly, trying to soften the weight of loneliness that he knew had settled on the boy's shoulders.

" I'll always be around in case ye're in *real* trouble— an' I'll know how ye're gettin' on. Ye'll be all right, Jim. Use yer head and do what ye're ordered to do to the best o' yer ability. Understand?"

" Yes," said Jim without enthusiasm. " I guess so, Patrick."

Utterly alone for the first time in his life, Jim made for the " I " company barrack room and reported to the first-sergeant.

First Sergeant Otto Schultz was a soldier from the soles of his gleaming cavalry boots to the utmost tip of his close-cropped blond hair. Of medium height, slim build, and with a complexion as tough and leathery as a pack saddle, he was as wiry and resilient as a steel spring. He had two prides : his German parentage, and his acknowledged ability to turn the rawest recruit into a hardened fighting man in the shortest possible time.

His first greeting left Jim in no doubt as to his character.

" So!" said Sergeant Schultz. " Now they send me babes an' sucklings with the cradle marks still on their backsides !"

Jim thought it better not to answer. He stood stiffly to attention and awaited the sergeant's next remarks.

" Name?"

" Peters, sir."

" Don't sir me, you ignorant greenhorn ! I'm not a perishin' officer."

" Nor ever will be," said a quiet voice with an edge of iron in it.

Sergeant Schultz whirled about, slamming to attention and saluting briskly as Captain Myles Keogh officer commanding " I " company, stepped through the doorway.

"Go to the regimental store and draw your uniform and kit," the captain ordered Jim. "Then report back to Sergeant Schultz. Go on, move! At the double!"

"Yessir!" Jim bolted for the door.

Captain Keogh turned to his company sergeant and regarded him soberly for a second or two. "Go easy with that one, Sergeant," he warned. "He's young, but he's already seen action against the Sioux."

Sergeant Schultz looked surprised. "Has he, sir?" he exclaimed. "Where was that?"

"The Black Hills. Colonel Custer told me himself—he hand-picked him, and you know as well as I do that the Colonel's never been wrong about a man or a boy yet. Keep your eye on him. You've got the makings of a soldier there."

"Yessir!" said Sergeant Schultz as the captain turned abruptly and left the barrack room. He waited for the footsteps to fade in the distance before he spoke again. "Officers!" he said sourly to the empty room. "They make me tired! I had that kid weighed up as my star pupil from the moment he set foot in this hut! It sticks out a mile!"

Oblivious to the conversation that was going on in the barrack room, Jim hurried to the regimental store and drew his kit.

Soon he was the proud possessor of such a mass of clothes and equipment that he couldn't for the life of him understand where he was going to stow it all.

Besides the uniform of dark blue blouse and trousers, field boots and campaign hat, there was a set of fatigue dress and garrison shoes, underwear, and a dress helmet for ceremonial parades. There was a mattress, two blankets, two pairs of socks, one pair of gloves, a rubber poncho or cape, a greatcoat and a forage cap.

"However much more do I get?" he asked the corporal clerk as he saw the pile of kit mounting higher and higher.

The corporal laughed. " I haven't started yet, son," he said. " There are another twenty items to sign for."

Jim thought he was having his leg pulled, but he had forgotten all the equipment for his personal use, his weapons and trappings, and the bridle, lariat, hobbles and picket pins for his horse.

" One Springfield carbine, one Colt revolver, ammunition for same, cartridge belt, saddlebags, water bottle, entrenching tool, sabre, sabre-sling, mess kit, razor, mirror, soap, comb . . ." on and on droned the storeman's voice as he added item after item to the pile.

" Nearly forgot the curry-comb," he apologised as he came to the end of the list, and double checked each item. " You'd be lost without that, son! That's the first thing you'll wear out in this outfit!"

" Thanks for the warning," Jim managed to smile. He collected up as much of his kit as he could manage to carry, and staggered back to the barrack room where Sergeant Schultz allocated him a bunk, showed him his locker, and detailed a trooper to help him stow his weapons and his kit in the approved fashion. Then he returned for the rest of the kit, filled his mattress with straw from the stable, and spent what was left of the morning learning all he could of the daily routine of a cavalry regiment from the friendly trooper.

" You'll shake down after the first week or two, Peters," he was told. " It takes a bit of gettin' used to, having every pip-squeak corporal and sergeant shoutin' at you from morning to night—but it's a good regiment, as regiments go."

" The best regiment in the American Army," echoed a voice from the far side of the barrack room, where a grey-haired veteran lay on his bunk nursing an injured arm that was encased in a grubby sling. "And I'll fight the first man as says different."

The next few days were a nightmare to Jim. He found himself roused out of his blankets by the blaring of Reveille at five-thirty. He joined the jostling crowd of grumbling men who all but fought for the privilege of being first at the ice-cold washing water, and learned to make a pretence of shaving the negligible growth of downy whiskers from his youthful cheeks. He learned to clean and polish his equipment, to march and counter march, to go through the motions of foot drill, rifle drill, sabre drill, and ceremonial drill. He knew the deadly monotony of cookhouse fatigue—sitting on a packing case for hours on end in front of a pile of potatoes which seemed never ending. He hauled timber and sawed logs for the cookhouse fires, cleaned out the barrack room, mounted guard with his troop, and slaved stripped to the waist on stable fatigue.

And that was only the beginning. He learned to darn his own socks, to mend his own clothes, and to stick up for his own rights when the other troopers tried to take advantage of him. He had his ears boxed, and his eyes blackened, and knew the indignity of being the youngest, rawest recruit in the regiment. And all the time the bugles shrilled at him from first light to sunset, blaring out their warning of fresh labours to come. He was shouted at, sworn at, told he was the most slovenly, inefficient, lazy, ignorant human being in the world. He was threatened, bullied, frightened, and awed in turn. But in spite of it all he still managed to smile, determined not to let Patrick O'Keefe down by any lapse, nor to let himself down by letting anyone see that he was as near to breaking point as it was possible to be.

If the truth were known, there were nights when hot tears formed in his eyes, and once or twice he buried himself deep under his blankets lest his rough and ready bunk-mates should hear the stifled sobs of loneliness and unhappiness that racked his toughening body. So also were there times when he felt he could not take another insult from a sneering corporal, or another piece of biting sarcasm from the ugly mouth of First Sergeant Schultz. He was sorely tempted to lash out at them with a tight balled fist. But he mastered all these weaknesses and impulses, and slowly, day by gruelling day, he felt himself becoming a man—a cavalryman.

In " C " company, where he had risen to the rank of guidon corporal—responsible for bearing the company's pennant on parade—Patrick O'Keefe followed Jim's progress with interest, and at times with concern. On his time off he kept carefully away from " I " company's barracks lest he should bump into Jim, but he went out of his way to cultivate friends among the non-commissioned officers and heard from them, in casual conversation, how the boy was shaping.

Colonel Custer too had his eye on Jim, though none but the shrewdest observer would have noticed. The Colonel prided himself on his memory for faces, and he soon picked out the gangling boy who had stood before him in his office from among the massed ranks of his command drawn up for inspection.

" How's your new bugler boy shaping, Keogh?" he asked one night at a social evening in the officers' mess. " It looks as though you're making a man of him."

Captain Keogh smiled. " He's got Sergeant Schultz to thank for that, Colonel. To tell the truth, sir, we neither of us want to make a bugler of him."

" Why?"

" He's got the makings of a first-rate sergeant in a few years' time," Captain Keogh explained. " May I ask why you're so interested in the boy, sir?"

Colonel Custer considered the question carefully,

stroking his fair moustache as he thought. "I'm blessed if I know, Keogh. There's something about his bearing, or his expression that tells me there's more to that lad than meets the eye. On top of that he was recommended by O'Keefe—and he's as good a judge as your Sergeant Schultz. If I'm right, that lad will be more use to the regiment as a bugler and special orderly than as a fighting trooper. We're going to need hand-picked, intelligent youngsters to act as couriers when we take the field."

Captain Keogh frowned. "Does that mean you think we have a campaign ahead of us, sir?" he asked seriously.

"I don't *think*, I know," said the commander. "It's only a question of time before the Sioux break out of the Reservation. Keep an eye on that lad—and any others you think are shaping well. We're going to need 'em."

"I will, sir," said Captain Keogh. "I think you're right."

"I am," said Colonel George Armstrong Custer as he moved off to welcome Major and Mrs. Reno and Captain and Mrs. Benteen to the gathering of his officers and their wives.

CHAPTER TEN

BUGLER TO THE SEVENTH

THE BAND of the Seventh Cavalry was the pride and joy of the regiment. Its repertoire included some twenty traditional marches and inspection pieces, ranging from "You're in the Army now" to "The Garrison Bells" and "Old Six-Eight." Whatever the occasion, the bandmaster had a lively tune to suit the mood, or to make the task of formal drilling easier.

Although principally a fife and drum band, it was augmented on most occasions by a corps of trumpeters and buglers, who puffed out their cheeks, pursed their lips, and added their brassy music to the lilting refrain of the regimental march—"Garry Owen."

They were practising this tune over and over again when Jim Peters reported to the band sergeant for his first lesson in blowing a bugle.

"When you can play like that, lad, you can call yourself a trumpeter," said Sergeant Brandt with a nod of his head in the direction of the red-faced musicians. "That's what constant practice does for you."

"Yes, Sergeant," said Jim, who had long ago learned always to agree with non-commissioned officers of all shapes, sizes and trades, from the cook-sergeant to the farrier-corporal.

"Not that you'll have to worry your head about real music," continued the band sergeant with a sigh of regret. "I've got instructions to teach you the rudiments o' bugling, an' the main calls of the day. Pick up that bugle over there and let's see how you shape."

At first Jim couldn't produce as much as a single,

fully-rounded note. He began to think that his bugle was stuffed with an old sock, or had been bent once too often when it was made. He blew, and blew, until his lips were numb and his cheeks ached, but he couldn't for the life of him produce anything resembling music.

And then, quite suddenly, he got the feel of the bugle and found the knack of shaping his notes before he blew. From then on there was no holding him. When he was not on band call he muted his bugle with a blanket and sat on his bunk for hours on end practising the notes he had been taught until he could hit the right ones every time. When his fellow troopers complained of the weird, strangled sighs that were welling up from beneath his blanket, he forsook barrack room practice and obtained permission from Sergeant Schultz to wander off to a stretch of waste land outside the fort where he could practise undisturbed.

So keen was he to master the bugle that in a matter of only a few weeks he was able to blow half a dozen calls perfectly, and a further half dozen passably.

" How many calls are there?" he asked Sergeant Brandt after his first few lessons.

" How many? Well now—around seventy recognised bugle calls," the instructor told him. " Not that we use them all—thank heavens."

" I should hope not!" Jim said with feeling. " I wouldn't learn all that lot in a month o' Sundays. Just how many will I have to know before you pass me out as a bugler?"

" Around thirteen, lad."

" Gee!" said Jim. " That's goin' to take a bit of doing!"

But it was really far easier than he thought. He mastered Reveille, Mess Call, Mail Call, Call to Quarters, Adjutant's Call, Assembly, General Call, Church Call and Drill Call, and managed to give a recognisable rendering of Tattoo and Taps. He learned to blow Retreat, and he also learned the duties of a bugler, in the field and on parade.

Almost before he realised it himself, he had become a fully trained bugler, and was entrusted with a place in the team who took it in turns to blow the calls of the day upon which the whole routine of the regimental headquarters depended.

There wasn't much fun in rolling out of bed, half an hour before any of the eight hundred men in the regiment, for the doubtful privilege of rousing them from their bunks with the strident, lively, dawn Reveille. There was less fun—in fact no fun at all—in knowing that Band Sergeant Brandt was lying in his blankets listening to every note he played with ears tuned to note each fault of tone or timing. There were many times when Jim wished he had never undertaken to learn the bugle—just as there had been times when he had regretted his decision to join the Army at all.

But despite all the drawbacks, Jim was happier than he had been for a long time. He had at last reached a stage in his career when he had a personal responsibility, and was no longer just another trooper among several hundred others. The entire complement of Fort Abraham Lincoln depended upon him to wake them, to warn them, to summon them to meals or drill, or any one of a dozen different duties. He rose to the responsibility gladly, and never once did he let the regiment down.

Perhaps the greatest joy at that time was the first Reveille Call he ever made. Standing shivering in the clammy cold of dawn, with the mist from the Missouri blotting out the distant shapes of the barracks buildings, Jim muttered an earnest prayer that he would make no mistakes. His eyes glued to the hands of a clock, he carefully cuddled the brass mouth-piece of his bugle in his gloved hand to warm the metal before raising it to his lips. The minute hand crept closer and closer to the half hour, and as it reached the mark he flung the bugle to his lips and let rip.

"Ta-rah-rah-rah-rah Ta-rah-rah-rah-rah Ta-rah-rah-rah-rah-rara."

It seemed that the sun had been waiting for his signal before it showed itself, for even as the last note of the first chorus died and Jim began again, the mist lifted, the sky lightened, and the clouds began to roll away. A light sprang into being from the cook-house window where a grumbling, grousing cook-corporal raked out a range and prepared to stoke up with logs in readiness for cooking breakfast for his company. Barrack room doors opened to reveal the forerunners of the yawning, scratching troopers who would soon be scurrying to the wash-houses.

And then, as Jim came to the end of his first duty call, he saw a familiar figure burst out of the sergeants' quarters, puffy-eyed with sleep, and muttering angrily to himself as he stood on the step and glowered at the "I" company barrack room which was his particular responsibility. Sergeant Schultz, who always prided himself on being up and about before the buglers, had overslept!

"Good-morning, Sergeant," Jim called out innocently as he passed Schultz on his way to his own quarters and breakfast.

"Bah!" said the First Sergeant, turning abruptly and slamming back into his hut.

If the Seventh Cavalry were proud of their band, they were prouder still of their horses. Jim had never seen such magnificent creatures before. They were a joy to ride, and even a pleasure to tend in their bare,

well-scrubbed stables. Along with his fellow troopers in
" I " company, he spent hours of every day curry-
combing, grooming, strawing and feeding the long lines
of prefectly-proportioned geldings.

There was great rivalry between the companies over
the appearance and the abilities of their horses—a
rivalry that was initiated and encouraged by Colonel
Custer himself.

"A cavalryman is only as good as his horse," the
commander of the Seventh Cavalry had been heard to
say to his officers. "I want the Seventh to be known
throughout the plains country for the quality of its
horseflesh. Give the men horses they can be proud of,
and you've already got the makings of a crack regiment."

Not everyone agreed with this viewpoint, and several
of the officers sneered at Custer behind his back. Chief
among the Colonel's detractors was the second-in-
command of the regiment, the dark-eyed, pot-bellied,
boasting Major Reno. "Poppycock!" he complained to
his friend Captain Benteen in the privacy of his own
quarters. "I've never heard such ridiculous nonsense
from a cavalry commander in all my career. It isn't
the horses that do the fighting—it's the men. Discipline
—firm, hard, relentless discipline—that's what makes
soldiers, and cavalry horses too."

Captain Benteen nodded his agreement. "It's a typi-
cal Custer remark," he grumbled. "Big talk, wild
statements, and showmanship. He can't forget his war
record. He wants to be leading a charge of hand-picked
horses and play-actor soldiers all the time. Anything to
add to his personal prestige and glamour. Pah! The
man's a menace on the frontier."

Whether it was jealousy of Custer's past rank and
personal glory, or whether there were real reasons for
distrusting the dare-devil exhibitionist commander of

the Seventh, it was difficult to say. All that was known was that "General" Custer was disliked—and even hated—by the majority of his officers. Jim Peters had sensed it in his first interview with Lt. Cooke, the Adjutant to the regiment, and he had long realised that it was the talk of the serving soldiers at Fort Abraham Lincoln.

But whatever the feeling of the officers towards their famous, unpredictable commanding officer, the fact remained that the troopers adored Custer to a man. Not only that, but they rose to his challenge over the question of their mounts like a fat river trout rising to snatch at a fisherman's fly. When they found that their horses were being inspected more carefully than themselves they strove to attract attention by a standard of personal smartness that had rarely been equalled by any regiment of fighting soldiers. They polished their brasses until they dazzled the eyes of the inspecting officers. They performed feats of horsemanship when manœuvring on the plains beyond the fort which caused even Custer's eyebrows to lift in surprise. As the standard of the horses improved—so did the pride and bearing of the men. It looked as though the "General" was right.

"I" company, of which Jim was now an accepted member, and a popular figure, had for their officer the stern-eyed Captain Keogh. A masterly horseman himself, the company commander had always insisted on choosing the horses for his troopers personally—long before Custer's sweeping statement. He had little love for the "General," thinking him conceited and unreliable, but he did have a certain respect for him, particularly over his judgment of men. But Captain Keogh accepted no man's judgment as being superior to his own when it came to horseflesh. He had an eye for horses, and he knew it.

"I want matched roans for my company, and

nothing else," he told the sutler, or camp trader, who supplied remounts to the regiment.

"Holy smoke!" said the sutler. "That's asking a lot, Captain!"

"Nonsense, man!" Captain Keogh retorted. "You supplied all greys to "E" company, an' by golly I'll have all roans!"

So it was that Jim Peters learned to soldier on some of the finest cavalry mounts in the regiment—all matched in colour, height and overall size; and all hand-picked with as much care as Captain Keogh had given to the choosing of his own horse—Comanche.

Comanche was a wonder horse. Jim knew it the moment he vaulted into his saddle and rode the beautiful roan across the parade ground to the farrier's forge for re-shoeing.

"Take good care of him, Peters," Captain Keogh warned, reluctant to see anyone but himself in the saddle of his favourite horse. "Use your spurs on him, or savage his mouth by hauling too hard on the curb, and I'll cut out your heart with my sabre—so help me!"

"No fear o' that, sir," Jim smiled, feeling the con-trolled power of the horse in its rippling muscles, and the proud arching of its neck. "I could ride my way to Heaven on Comanche, an' never know I was movin'!"

Captain Keogh's face broke into a rare smile. "You know horseflesh, youngster," he nodded approvingly. "I'll get you to exercise Comanche for me sometime."

"Yes *sir*!" said Jim with delight.

He was returning from the forge, with Comanche stepping gingerly after the cutting and trimming of his hooves, as though he wasn't quite used to the unaccus-tomed weight of the new shoes, when Patrick O'Keefe crossed the parade ground ahead of him.

"Mornin' Corporal!" Jim called.

Patrick O'Keefe turned in his saddle, recognised Jim, and swung his horse towards him, his face beaming with pleasure.

"What are ye doin' on Comanche?" the Irishman asked. "Captain Keogh's mighty jealous o' that horse."

"He's asked me to exercise him," Jim told his old friend casually, as though it was a commonplace assignment.

"Has he?" Patrick whistled. "Looks as though ye're findin' yer feet in the regiment, me bucko!"

Jim grinned. "I guess I am," he said modestly. "Perhaps I'll soon be allowed to mix with guidon corporals from 'C' company." He couldn't resist the dig at Patrick, whose two yellow inverted stripes showed glaringly against the dark blue of his fatigue blouse.

The Irishman smiled. "Maybe," he acknowledged with a chuckle. "But if it's meself ye're referrin' to, Jim, ye'll be too late after to-day."

Jim was mystified. "Why?" he asked with a frown.

"Because as from to-morrow Guidon Corporal Patrick O'Keefe is promoted sergeant—an' transferred to 'I' company. Ye'll be takin' orders from me to-morrow, me bucko!"

"No!" said Jim.

"Yes!" contradicted Sergeant Patrick O'Keefe as he swung away with a wave of his hand and a gurgle of laughter. "Ye'd better watch out—I'm known as a holy terror when I get the bit between me teeth!"

CHAPTER ELEVEN

SCOUTING PARTY

JIM VIEWED Patrick O'Keefe's posting to his own company with mixed feelings.

It would be pleasant to have the laughing Irishman close at hand after all the long months of only seeing him from a distance, but it would also tend to make life difficult for them both. Patrick would have to watch himself very carefully lest he should be accused of favouritism towards Jim; and the young bugler would himself have to make sure he didn't overstep the rigid code of etiquette which governed personal friendship of a ranker with a non-commissioned officer.

As it happened, Jim had little to worry about, for Patrick was too experienced a sergeant not to know how to deal with what could have been a tricky situation. Not only that, but the newly-made sergeant had been posted to " I " company with a reason—a reason that wasn't divulged to him until he had been with the company three days. It was also going to have a big effect upon Jim Peters' career.

The first Jim knew of it was when he was told to report to Captain Keogh in person. He arrived to find Patrick O'Keefe standing rigidly to attention in front of the company commander—and Colonel Custer!

" Gather round this map," the Colonel ordered after Jim had saluted and been told to stand easy. " I've got important work for you two."

With a mounting sense of excitement Jim found himself staring at a large-scale map of the plains country, stretching from Fort Reno, north, to the Yellowstone river. Westwards the foothills of the Rockies were covered, while to the east the Black Hills were etched in red to show the outline of the Sioux Reservation.

"I had you released from company duty with 'C' company and transferred to 'I' with this assignment in view," Colonel Custer continued with a shrewd glance at Patrick. "You are to scout this area." He tapped the map to indicate the Sioux buffalo grounds in the basin of the Yellowstone, and between the Powder and the Big Horn tributaries. "Captain Keogh is providing three sound men to ride with you, and Peters here is attached to you as special courier."

Jim's heart gave a leap. "Special courier!" he thought. "What does that mean?" He wasn't to be kept in the dark for long.

"What are my orders, sorr?" Patrick asked.

Colonel Custer chose his words with care. "You are to scout this area with the greatest possible thoroughness," he said. "I want as much information as you can give me regarding the movement of Sioux hunting parties. I want to know their size, their whereabouts, and a report of any contact they have with each other or with the Reservation. Understand?"

"Yes, sorr." Patrick hesitated before following with a question. "What is the object o' this scout, sorr?" he asked.

Colonel Custer leaned back in his chair. "Your report will go straight to Washington, Sergeant," he said with deliberate emphasis. "On its accuracy depends what action the Government takes to restrict the movements of the Sioux." He stopped as a frown passed over Patrick's face. "Let me explain further," he continued. "The more you know, the more you will realise how important this patrol is. Sit down, both of you, and listen."

Jim took a seat across the table from Custer and listened as though his life depended upon it. Patrick sank down beside him, the leather of his uniform belt creaking as he moved his stout body.

"As you know," Custer went on, "the Sioux are allowed to hunt buffalo on the plains outside the Reservation during certain months of the year. That was agreed in the Treaty of Fort Laramie. Now, we have reason to believe that as a result of the trouble up in the Black Hills, which you both experienced, there is growing unrest among both the Cheyennes under Dull Knife, and the Sioux under Sitting Bull. We have heard rumour that envoys are passing among the hunting parties. Their object is to encourage the braves to stay out on the plains, and to persuade more and more braves to join them from the Reservation. If this is true, we cannot, *dare not,* allow it."

"This sounds like Sittin' Bull's work," Patrick put in.

Custer nodded. "We believe it is, O'Keefe. He is diabolically clever. He knows that any mass break-out from the Reservation would be met at once by all the might of the Plains Armies, so instead he gets his braves to dribble out in small bands, so that their coming and going is hardly noticed. Then, once they are out in sufficient numbers to prove a serious threat to the peace of the settlements, he refuses to allow them to return. The break-out is complete without a shot being fired."

". . . and instead of having them bottled up on the Reservation where we can control them by force, if necessary, they are scattered all over the territory so that it would take three times the number of soldiers to keep them under!"

"Exactly!" said Colonel Custer, as he rose to his feet. "So you will see, O'Keefe, that you have to move fast, scout thoroughly, and get back with your report in double-quick time. That's why I'm providing you with a special courier."

"Yes, sorr," said Patrick, springing to his feet as the Colonel rose, with Jim only a second or two behind him.

"Right. Captain Keogh will give you detailed orders and make all the necessary arrangements. You are under his orders from now on."

Colonel Custer strode to the door, acknowledging the salutes of the captain and the two men. He paused in the doorway, turned, and smiled. "Good luck, O'Keefe —and to you Peters. I shall depend upon you."

"Thank you, sir!" Patrick and Jim chorused.

When Custer had gone Captain Keogh lost no time in getting down to the relevant details of the fast-moving scouting patrol.

"You'll live off the land as far as possible, Sergeant," he informed Patrick. "I have arranged for iron rations, but don't touch them unless you have to. I'm more concerned with the quantity of grain you can carry to keep the horses in condition than I am with food for your party."

Patrick nodded. "That's good sense, Captain," he agreed. "I was going to suggest that if ye hadn't."

"The three men I am detailing to go with you are first-class veterans. They all know the plains country as well as you do, Sergeant. They are Larkin, Thomson and Siggers. They are checking over their horses right now."

"When do we start, Captain?" Patrick asked.

"First light to-morrow. You must have all your preparations complete to-night, Sergeant. I'll inspect your patrol immediately before supper, and remember, no word of your mission to anyone. Understand?"

"Yes, sorr."

"Right. If there are no other questions you may dismiss."

Saluting, Patrick and Jim turned to go. Captain Keogh's voice stopped Jim as he thudded after Patrick over the boarded floor.

"Peters!"

"Yessir!"

"You'll need the fastest and the best horse you can lay your hands on. Have you any particular preference?"

Before he realised what he was saying, Jim blurted out: "Comanche, sir."

For a moment he thought that Captain Keogh was going to strike him. For a mere bugler to suggest that he took the captain's personal mount on a hard-riding scouting mission among possible hostiles! Jim didn't know what had come over him to say such a thing. He heard Patrick grunt with amazement—and then Captain Keogh found his voice.

"If I didn't know you better, Peters, I would say that that was the grossest impertinence I've ever heard!" his company commander spluttered.

Jim held himself rigid—expecting to be put under close arrest at the very least. Impertinence to an officer was just about the most serious crime in a trooper's life. "I'm s-s-sorry, sir," he stammered. "I wasn't thinking. Comanche has been on my mind ever since you said I could exercise him. His name just kinda s-s-slipped out, sir!"

"So you like my horse?" There was a strange intonation about the question, and Jim didn't quite know how to answer.

"No one who knows horses could help but like him, sir," he said with simple honesty. "He's a hum-dinger of a horse. He's a bit skittish at the moment, but that's because he hasn't been worked much. He wants working, badly. Then he could beat any other horse in the regiment, sir."

Captain Keogh picked up some papers from his desk. He straightened up and looked Jim in the eyes. There was a little darting light deep in the pupils. Was it? Could it be . . . a twinkle?

"That's just what I was saying to Sergeant Schultz this morning,"the company commander said. "Look after him, Peters. Comanche will enjoy this patrol—and he might even teach you a thing or two."

"You mean . . .?" Jim could hardly believe his ears.

"Yes. Comanche is yours for the duration of this patrol. Dismiss!"

"Yes, sir!" said Jim, saluting so vigorously that he practically knocked his cap off.

Jim Peters knew all three of the troopers who had been detailed to accompany Patrick and himself on Custer's mission. They were "I" company men, and Seventh Cavalry veterans with at least eight years' plains experience behind them. There wasn't much they didn't know about horses, men, or Indians.

Meeting the troopers for the first time, Patrick was immediately impressed by their bearing. He was not at all surprised to find that they all had a good idea of the purpose of their mission. They had as keen an understanding of the Sioux problem as their Colonel.

"It's as plain as the nose on my face," Thomson said as they rode out of the Fort at dawn with their meagre rations safely stowed in the leather pouches, and grain for the horses strapped securely to their saddles. "The Sioux have been building up for real trouble these past ten months and more—even before the miners slipped into the Black Hills."

Larkin agreed. "We'll be campaigning before the winter's out," he commented grimly.

Patrick let them talk as they rode. "Let them get it off their chests," he thought. "Once they have aired their views they'll settle down to the job in hand." Sure enough they fell silent after they had travelled some five miles, and barely spoke for the rest of the morning. The pace Patrick O'Keefe set with his big, awkward-looking bay was enough to make even the most experienced horseman conserve both his breath and his energy for the exertion of riding.

Mounted on Comanche, Jim Peters was in his seventh heaven. He had never ridden such a horse. He appeared to glide over the roughest of the terrain with long, effortless strides, breathing easily, tossing his head in pleasure at being out on the open range after so long within the confines of the fort, his great hooves pounding at the turf in the same mile-eating gait, hour after hour.

"What a horse!" Jim kept saying to himself, over and over again, and it was as though Comanche heard and understood for he tossed his head proudly, flicking his ears, and allowing his light-coloured mane to flow out to one side in the wind of his own progress. By every little gesture and movement he showed his approval of the light-weight, firm-handed rider on his back. Even Siggers, the third trooper, who had shown his undisguised jealousy at Jim's unusual honour of riding the captain's horse, was the first to admit secretly to himself that Comanche and the young bugler made a perfect combination. It was as though they were welded together in one piece—half horse and half man.

They halted at noon, many miles from Fort Abraham Lincoln, and with the wide Missouri showing far below them, with a river steamer anchored at the jetty looking like a toy floating on a ribbon of silver paper. They ate slowly, walking about to ease their cramped thighs, and to shake out the stiffness of their joints.

At night they camped under the stars, without bothering to build bivouacs. Rolled in their blankets, and protected from the damp of earth and sky by rubber ponchos, they slept soundly—their horses hobbled by the forelegs, and confined by thirty feet of lariat tied to their bridles and pegged to the ground by a picket pin.

It was on the third day that they saw their first sign of the Sioux. Larkin had been sent forward to scout the further side of a rolling ridge of scrub-covered country before the others came up. Waiting in their saddles, the others saw him approach the skyline cautiously, on foot, and peer over to whatever lay beyond.

Seconds later Larkin had darted back behind cover, flapping his arms in signal of alarm. He seized his horse by the bridle, held his hand firmly over its muzzle to prevent it whinnying, and led it down the slope to where Patrick waited.

"Sioux," Larkin said briefly as he reached the sergeant. "I durned near walked slap into them!"

"How many?"

"Ten to fifteen lodges, Sarge. Women, kids, young an' old. Cooking fires goin' full blast. They must've had a big kill o' buff'lo."

Patrick grunted. "Take the others round to the north, Larkin," he ordered. "Keep out o' sight, an' make camp in that stand o' timber. I'm goin' forward with Peters—it's time he learned to identify one tribe from another. He's only seen hostiles before—at the end o' a rifle barrel!"

"If you ask me, Sarge, that's the only way to look at a Sioux!" said Larkin with feeling.

"I didn't ask ye," said Patrick O'Keefe curtly.

CHAPTER TWELVE

THE MEDICINE CHIEF

LYING THERE in the scrub of the ridge Jim Peters' mind was in a turmoil. The sight of a whole village of Sioux busying themselves about their everyday tasks right under his nose had come as something of a shock to him.

For months now the youngster had been putting all thought of his bitter experience up in the Black Hills far to the back of his mind. He had tried to shut out all memory of the death of his Uncle Moses, and of that dreadful twenty minutes when the gorge where their claim lay had been filled with the war cries of painted savages, the acrid smell of exploding powder, and the terrified neighs of the horses.

Now, as he looked at the peaceful scene below him, with squaws and little children chattering excitedly, laughing and singing and playing games around the tepees, the death of his uncle at the hands of the Sioux seemed completely unreal—as though it had happened in a horrible nightmare.

Could these innocent, laughing people be the same as the murdering youths who had ridden to their death in the gorge? Were they the dreaded Sioux—the most warlike tribe of all the plains Indians? Were these the same Indians whom Trooper Larkin and a thousand other soldiers like him swore were no better than vermin, to be exterminated as though they were rats in a warehouse?

Jim couldn't believe it. And yet in the back of his

mind was a hatred of the red savages who had killed his uncle and driven Patrick and him from their mine: a hatred and a fear of all redmen. He didn't know what to think.

Glancing at the boy, Patrick O'Keefe read the thoughts that were whirling about in his mind.

"Those are Uncpapa Sioux—Sittin' Bull's own tribe," the Irishman said in a whisper. "See the markin's on their tepees, an' the trappin's on the horses. Mark them well, an' remember them, lad. They are the aristocrats o' all the Indians—an' like all aristocrats they're mighty proud."

"They . . . they . . . look so . . . so . . . *peaceful*!" Jim stammered

Patrick nodded. "They do, lad. They're happy when they're out on the plains with buffalo to hunt, an' work to do. But they can change into murderin', torturin' devils in seconds if their pride is hurt—the women just as bad or worse than the men. Sittin' Bull took a whippin' from Custer months an' months ago. He was wise enough to know when he was beaten—but he hasn't forgotten. He's only bidin' his time."

"Then what?" asked Jim.

"Then he'll do his durnedest to play on the pride o' his own people, an' the pride o' the Ogallalas, the Cheyennes, an' every last one o' the Plains tribes. He'll have them whipped into a frenzy o' killin' an' fightin' just as sure as there's a sun in the sky. A Sioux always gets revenge. Remember that, an' don't ever be fooled by them. The 'General' knows it better than anyone. That's why we're up here."

"To judge when the time has come?" asked Jim as his thoughts began to clear.

"Yes, lad. Custer knows the Army has got to move first—at the critical moment. Then we've got Sittin' Bull beaten before he starts, an' before there's almighty bloodshed. Remember what I told ye about soldierin'?"

"Yes, Patrick. You said that Custer an' men like him worked to *stop* killing—that soldiers were used to enforce peace, not to make war."

"That's it," the veteran sergeant said approvingly. "An' right now ye're takin' part in a battle o' wits between Custer—or Yellowhair as the Sioux call him—an' Sittin' Bull."

"Who's going to win?" Jim asked as the full importance of their mission was revealed to him.

Patrick shrugged. "Yer guess is as good as mine, Jim. What worries me is that the 'General' hasn't got half the patience Sittin' Bull has. He's a man o' action—a fighter. When his dander's up there's no holdin' him."

"Then . . ." Jim began.

"Then the Seventh Cavalry stand a good chance o' stirrin' up the biggest hornets' nest o' all time," Patrick finished for him.

The Sioux encampment was only the first of many they were to encounter in the next ten days of hard riding, long gruelling hours in the saddle, and careful, thorough scouting.

They came upon small bands of but a few lodges, isolated families, and large massed groups consisting of a mixture of three or four sections of the Sioux race— each one distinct, with its own carefully observed camp site, and yet all members of the great Sioux Nation.

Jim took his turn at forward scouting, learning to fade into the barest cover at a minute's notice when the whiff of wood-smoke, or the odour of smouldering buffalo-chip fires came to him over the fresh, rain-filled air of early autumn.

They crossed and re-crossed the plains, working their

way through luxuriant, waist-high grasses, and across close-cropped turfy valleys where the buffalo had fed through the long, blazing days of summer. They struck belts of dense woodland that slowed their progress and kept them on constant, nervy watch for what lay hidden ahead of them. They forded streams, wide tributaries of the Yellowstone, and skirted marshy, reed-covered bogs. At times they found themselves peering down upon the Indian buffalo hunting camps from the height of rocky ridges—at other times they saw the redmen cross the skyline above them with their rolled tepees trailing behind their horses on the lashed poles of travois sledges.

Everywhere they went they met with the same sight; the Sioux were pre-occupied with hunting, with killing the great snorting, stupid, short-sighted animals that were their natural prey. They saw massed braves riding into the herds to hunt on bareback mustangs which were dwarfed by the mighty bull buffalo. They saw them kill with bow and arrow, trade musket, lance and, rarely, with modern high-powered rifles they had bought or bartered, or stolen from the white men.

A dozen times Jim watched the rapid skinning of the still warm carcasses. The braves worked with amazing speed and skill to peel the thick, supple hides and hand them to the squaws for scraping, cleaning, and dressing so that they could be turned into warm, durable robes or tepee covers. He watched as the huge joints of meat were sliced and butchered for the immediate needs of the tribe, for smoking over herb-fed fires, or for the preparation of pemmican and other winter delicacies. He noted how the horns and hooves were saved for making powder flasks, drinking vessels, and ornaments. He learned how the redmen never wasted the smallest piece of a carcass, using sinews for bow-strings, paunches for water carriers and bones for hammers, clubs or toys for the children.

All this he and his companions saw time and time again, fascinated by the concentrated industry of the warriors as they prepared for the long winter months ahead without thought to the " White Eyes" who watched and spied upon them.

Everywhere the troopers rode they found the same thing—the Sioux were preoccupied with hunting. They were not contemplating war, or even allowing themselves to think of anything but the job in hand. The buffalo were all-important to them.

" Guess we've got all the information we're seeking, haven't we, Sarge?" asked Larkin on the morning of the thirteenth day.

" It looks that way," Patrick agreed. " But I'm not happy. I can't shake off a hunch that we're missin' something."

" I've got the same feelin'," Siggers said quietly. " Things are too durned peaceful, if you ask me, Sarge. If the buffalo weren't runnin' so free up here those pesky Injuns would be sittin' around, moonin' over their pipes an' talkin' war."

" That's just it!" Patrick exclaimed. " I shan't be happy we've seen the full picture o' the tribes until we find a village where the huntin' is over an' done with, an' the braves have time for talk. We'll stick around for another coupla days an' see what we can find."

" You're the boss," said Larkin, but it was plain from his tone that he thought a prolonged scout was valueless. He was already eyeing the changing weather with concern, and wished that he was back in the warmth and shelter of Fort Abraham Lincoln.

" I am, *Trooper*," said Patrick icily. He didn't like Larkin—that was clear.

It was on the following day that Jim spotted the smoke of the distant fires. He slipped his regulation Springfield carbine from the scarred leather scabbard forward of his right leg, and held it high above his head—the muzzle pointing in the direction of the smoke. Patrick O'Keefe caught on at once.

"The boy's on to somethin'," he called to the three troopers. "Let's get up there, fast!"

The smoke proved to be what they had been seeking. It came from the site of a large encampment in the hollows beside a slow-flowing, shallow stream. Eyeing it through glasses, Patrick knew at once that this was an important camp, a chiefs' camp. Three prominent, specially-marked lodges stood out like sore thumbs, grouped round a large medicine lodge.

"Make camp," he ordered. "I'll go ahead by myself. We'll be spotted if we all go. They're bound to have scouts out with chiefs present."

Larkin and Thomson dismounted and began to lead their horses into the cover of nearby trees. Siggers remained mounted. "It's none o' my business, Sarge," he said hesitantly, "but if I were you I'd take Peters with you. He's the courier. If the Sioux jump you he's the one who has to report to the 'General.' It would be best if he knew what you had seen."

Patrick O'Keefe frowned. He wasn't used to having his thinking done for him, by a trooper. Then he remembered that Siggers had had more experience of the plains than any of them, and he saw the sense of what he had suggested. "I think ye're right, Trooper," he acknowledged. "If anything happens to me see that the boy hot-foots it to the 'General' without delay. Give him cover if the Sioux ride after him— then break off and make for the Fort."

"Orders heard and understood, Sergeant," Siggers answered smartly as he swung his horse after his companions—pleased with the way his suggestion had been received.

The sun was setting as Patrick and Jim wormed

their way through the trees surrounding the camp and studied the terrain with the utmost caution. They had left their horses way back in a thicket where the chances of them being discovered were practically nil, and had covered a good mile on foot.

It was clear that they were about to witness an important pow-wow. A large fire had been lighted in the centre of a wide, level stretch of ground in front of the principal lodge. They could sense the buzz of excitement that was in the air around the village of tepees. Squaws busied themselves with elaborate cooking preparations, turning deer and buffalo meat on greenwood spits, basting whole duck and quail, and stirring highly spiced concoctions in huge iron cooking pots.

The younger boys were gathered round the horse herd, looking sulky and bad-tempered.

" 'They're wild at missin' the pow-wow an' the feast-in'," Patrick chuckled in Jim's ear. " Horse mindin' is an old man's job—but when there's a meetin' o' the elders o' the tribe, the kids have to take over. This is goin' to be mighty interestin'."

" Dare we get any closer?" Jim whispered back.

Patrick glanced about. " I guess so," he said eventually. " There aren't any guards. Everyone seems too interested in gettin' fixed up in finery an' feathers to bother their heads about us."

Slowly, moving as silently as snakes, they wriggled closer and closer, until they reached the cover of two large rocks, within fifty yards of the rear of the medicine lodge.

" Wonderful," sighed Patrick. " Give a sneeze or a cough, an' by the sainted banks o' Killarney, I'll have ye court-martialled, Jim!"

Jim grinned back in the gathering darkness, but he wasn't feeling very happy. To tell the truth he was downright scared. His heart beat a steady thumping tattoo against his ribs, and he had already regretted suggesting to Patrick that they should crawl nearer to the lodges. Every time a flame leaped in the big council fire he felt sure that they would be discovered.

All this time the braves and the old men had been gathering from every corner of the camp. Senior members of the tribe could be seen moving towards the inner circle of the council with slow, dignified strides. Dressed in the finest, softest doeskin, ornamented with porcupine quills and beads sewn in intricate patterns and tribal symbols, they took their rightful places. Jim noticed that they were careful not to pass between any man and the council fire, for that would have been an insult, and a breach of the strict Sioux etiquette. They passed behind, bowing to the elders, and taking the greatest possible care not to offend by any gesture or movement the ritual assembly of braves and warriors and chiefs.

Each member of the inner circle of the council had his specially appointed place, allotted to him by virtue of his seniority in the tribe, his prowess in battle, or by his leadership of any one of the half dozen secret societies which flourished within the tribe.

Some represented the warrior societies—the hard core of skilled and experienced full-time guards and defenders of the tribe. Others bore the emblems of the hunting societies—that exclusive band of Indians renowned for their abilities in leading the daily search for food, and responsible for the feeding and clothing of the entire tribe. There were the leaders of the tribal police, whose duties were the enforcement of the chief's orders for the welfare of the men, women and children in his charge.

There were the highly honoured craftsmen of the tribe—the makers of the finest, truest arrows, the strongest bows, and the sharpest tomahawks and knives.

There were men who could perform unbelievable feats of skill in metalwork, in wood, or bone, or leather. Each had some carefully assessed standing and respect within the council of the tribe, and each had his own alloted place of honour.

These men, the leaders of the everyday life of the tribe, were dressed and adorned according to their importance. Some wore the flowing head-dresses of goose and eagle feathers, dyed in shades of yellow, green or vermilion; others sported two or three colour-tipped feathers. All wore their straight black hair in long Sioux braids, hanging down on either side of their proud aristocratic faces and falling well below their shoulders. Oiled and greased, the braids glistened in the firelight, denoting the care with which the preparations for the council had been made.

Jim Peters lay behind the rocks, fascinated by it all. He was particularly interested in the faces of the Sioux elders. They were nothing like white men's faces, nor were they like the faces of the Rees and the Crow Indians who served as scouts with the Army. They resembled neither the Apaches he had seen photographed in the eastern newspapers, nor the bloodthirsty Comanches he had seen once on a trip to the south. They were distinctive—Sioux faces, slant-eyed, with high cheek bones, wide full lips, and proud hawklike noses. Strength and courage and intelligence showed plainly in every line and feature, and in the faces of the old men of the tribe there was even kindness, humour, and wisdom etched clearly for all to see.

Behind these men the young warriors, the onefeather braves, and the young bucks of the tribe were forming up. They were vastly different in attitude, in character, and in bearing. They positively strutted, with all the arrogance of their youth, vying with each other to be noticed by the squaws and maidens who hovered in the background.

These were the dangerous members of the tribe. The young warriors who had yet to prove themselves, and who had yet to learn the wisdom, patience and self-control of their elders. They were the ones unscrupulous war-chiefs could whip into a frenzy—they were the ones who cared nothing for death, but everything for glory.

It was untried, glory-seeking boys like these who had killed Moses Peters, and a wave of uncontrollable hatred welled up within his nephew as he saw them and read them for what they were.

"Murdering devils!" he gritted from between clenched teeth, understanding now how Trooper Larkin felt about the redmen.

"Shh!"

Patrick O'Keefe put a warning finger to his lips.

"Do ye want us both killed?" he whispered fiercely.

Jim controlled his feelings, regretting his unintentional outburst, and feeling he had let Patrick down by allowing his emotions to get the better of him.

At that moment a strange hush fell upon the Indians who now squatted cross-legged on the firelit ground. The flap of the medicine lodge was flung back, and a short, thick-set Indian stepped into view with his back to the rocks where Jim and Patrick lay.

Dressed in a simple costume of the softest, whitest doeskin Jim had ever seen, the redman was obviously a medicine chief of superior standing. Not for him the gaudy finery of trailing head-dress and ornamented clothes—he was above such trifles, a man who knew that his power and strength were in his knowledge, his wisdom, and the soundness of his counsel, and of his judgment.

With solemn dignity the bareheaded, stocky Indian moved forward to the fire. Gradually, inch by inch, he raised his arms high above his head, widespread, invoking the blessing of the Great Manitou himself upon the council of the tribe. He retraced his steps without turning, drew forth a long large-bowled pipe, lighted it with a burning brand, and held it high. Then, with great solemnity, he offered it first to the north, then to the south, then east, then west—to the Four Winds, and to the Great Spirit of the Plains.

Bowing low to the council fire, he took his position of honour at the right hand of the tribal chief. He turned, passing the smouldering council pipe to his neighbour —and Patrick O'Keefe jerked with surprise.

"Holy sufferin' catfish!" he gasped. "It's Sittin' Bull himself!"

CHAPTER THIRTEEN

" COMANCHE "

SITTING BULL, medicine chief of all the Sioux, spoke
for the best part of an hour in the guttural, jerky, language of his tribe. He was heard out in silence by the
full council and the young braves—and by Jim Peters,
who didn't understand a single word of what was being
said.

But Patrick O'Keefe knew the Sioux tongue well.
What he learned caused him to frown and mutter under
his breath. Jim, fighting against his growing impatience
to know what was going on, was hard put to hold his
peace.

"What's he saying?" he demanded in the barest
whisper.

Patrick silenced him with an angry gesture, and as
the long minutes dragged by, mounting into a quarter
of an hour, half an hour, and finally a full hour of
unintelligible talk, Jim stirred restlessly, doing his best
to stifle the yawns that threatened to break from his
mouth.

At last the medicine man's harangue came to an end.
The sub-chiefs added their views and conclusions to the
council of their elders, and the arguments began. Jim
tried to concentrate on the tone of the voices which
made the long, involved speeches, in the hope that they
would give some clue to what was being said. Soon he
came to the definite conclusion that nearly all the
elders were impressed and persuaded by the power of
Sitting Bull's argument, whilst the younger braves, and
the warrior chiefs, were violently opposed to what the
medicine chief advocated.

As the young warriors spoke, Jim glanced across to Patrick, and saw the sergeant's frown deepen. That seemed to back up his reading of the situation, and when, ten minutes later, Patrick signed to him to leave the shelter of the rocks and make for the woods, he was convinced that he was right.

Once in the safety of the trees, Patrick O'Keefe wasted no words.

"Listen, lad," he urged. "Listen closely an' remember every word. Ye must ride ahead at once an' take this news to the 'General' as fast as ye can."

"What shall I tell him?"

"Tell him that Sittin' Bull is tourin' every principal camp out on the plains. He is advisin' every last one o' the Sioux an' Cheyenne tribes to stay away from the Reservation when the huntin' is over. He says that the Reservation is nothin' but a white man's trap. The Sioux are being penned in, an' year by year the white men squeeze them a little tighter. This year it is gold that makes the White Eyes encroach upon the Sioux lands. Next year it will be hunters who will rob the Injuns o' their buffalo. The year after it will be somethin' else—an' all the time the Sioux will be driven closer an' closer together, until they starve for lack of food an' lack o' space."

Patrick paused for breath. "Got that?" he asked.

"Yes," Jim told him. "That's just what the 'General' expects to hear. Was there anything else?"

"Sure. Plenty. Tell Custer that the warriors an' the youngsters want to make a fight of it straight away. They say it will come to it in the end, so why not now? They are all for war before the winter."

"What did Sitting Bull have to say about that?"

"He said let the Army do the attackin' if they want to. They would find the Sioux ready for them. The elders agreed with him."

"Is that all?" Jim asked, impatient to start his ride after the long spell of inactivity.

"Not quite," Patrick said with grim emphasis. "Tell the 'General' that it's clear the Sioux are spoilin' for a fight. Tell Custer that the time has come to move, an' move fast. Sittin' Bull has been feedin' war talk to those braves, all hidden up in talk o' patience. What he's after is to provoke the Army into an attack. Then every last Sioux, young an' old, will be behind him in an all-out war."

"Gee! He's cunning all right!" Jim exclaimed. "It's just like you said it would be, Patrick."

Patrick O'Keefe nodded. "The 'General' will have to move fast if he aims to prevent bloodshed, Jim. He's got to order the Sioux back to their Reservation before Sittin' Bull has a chance to persuade them to stay out. It's a race against time—an' from what we've seen to-night Sittin' Bull is way ahead already!"

It wasn't until Jim Peters settled down to that fast, practically non-stop ride back to Fort Abraham Lincoln that he appreciated fully the wisdom of Captain Keogh in allowing him to take Comanche. No other horse could have stood the pace after weeks of riding throughout the rolling plains country.

It was as though Comanche sensed the importance of the verbal report that his young rider carried. Getting into his full, long-legged stride he thundered over the prairie land—revelling in the power and strength of his rippling muscles, and the stoutness of his lungs. There was no holding him once he had outdistanced the other horses. Jim gave up all thought of holding him. He let the reins go slack and contented himself with easing Comanche's burden by riding with the utmost skill at his command.

Patrick O'Keefe had relieved Jim of his carbine, his

scabbard, and all the surplus kit, in the hope that the few pounds of weight saved would enable the courier to travel faster. Like all cavalrymen, the Irish sergeant knew that an Army horse hated the nagging slap of a leather scabbard against its belly, just as it resented the rattle and jingle of fancy harness and accoutrements. Stripped to the barest essentials, any horse would respond by a greater effort, and Comanche was no exception to the rule. By noon the sergeant and his three troopers were out of sight, and the exultant bay showed no sign of flagging.

On and on they sped, stopping for only the briefest spells to drink, to snatch a hurried meal, and to rest. Then it was saddle and ride again in silent concentration, without thought to the country they were passing through, or of the ever-changing autumn weather. It was as though a bond existed between the bay gelding and his rider—a bond of mutual trust and understanding. They worked together as a team, closing their eyes and ears, and even their thoughts, to everything other than the speed of their journey, and the urgency of the report for the commander of the Seventh Cavalry.

At last, weary to the point of exhaustion, but still gamely plodding on through the mud and ruts of the riverside trail, they came to the shadows of the fort and checked at the lamplit guardhouse.

"Courier for Colonel Custer!" Jim called out, his voice harsh and croaking with fatigue.

The duty sergeant held his lamp high, recognised horse and rider, and passed them through into the fort with a gesture.

By now Comanche was all in, and Jim was little better. They made their way slowly across the parade ground, heading for the lighted window of the Adjutant's office, where the duty officer was to be found.

Comanche came to a shuffling halt, and Jim slid

down from the saddle with a groan of relief. His thighs ached, and his muscles throbbed. It was as much as he could do to put one foot before the other, but he paused by Comanche's side and patted the drooping arch of his neck, feeling the damp stickiness of lather and the grit of mud and sand.

"Well done, old feller. Well done," he murmured.

Comanche swung his tired head, nuzzling the dirty roughness of Jim's blouse, and snuffling through his nostrils—too tired to raise even the suggestion of a whinny.

Jim reached up, slipped the reins over Comanche's head to trail in the dust of the parade ground, and mounted the steps to the office.

Five minutes later the duty officer was hammering on the door of Colonel Custer's quarters, with Jim, half asleep on his feet, standing beside him.

Custer himself came to the door, flinging it wide, demanding angrily who in tarnation wanted him at this hour of the night.

"Courier from the scouting party, sir," announced the duty officer stiffly. "I thought it my duty to rouse you at once, Colonel."

Colonel Custer's attitude changed immediately. "The courier!" he cried. "Good! Of course you did right, Lieutenant—show him in at once!"

"He's all in, sir," the lieutenant cautioned as the commander bent to squint down at Jim's swaying body.

"I can see that, man!" Custer retorted testily. "Quick, carry him into the house while I fetch the brandy bottle. I *must* have his report to-night. I leave for Washington in the morning!"

All this Jim heard as though in a dream. All he wanted to do was to sleep and sleep and sleep. He felt himself being lifted bodily from the ground and carried inside. His brain kept telling him that he must keep his eyes open at all costs, but try as he would they kept closing. He found himself being laid down gently on the Colonel's sitting-room couch. He felt a glass at his lips, and a burning, biting liquid hit his tongue, making him cough and choke. Miraculously his head cleared, he sat up, and tried to struggle to his feet, his hand already moving up in an attempt to salute.

" Be still, boy," came Custer's voice, and a firm but kindly hand pushed him back on to the couch. Then : " All right, Lieutenant. You may go now. He'll revive in a minute or two."

" Yessir !"

Jim heard the thud of the duty officer's heels as he saluted, and the smart, small-stepped strides as the lieutenant crossed the room and left the Colonel and himself alone. He blinked his eyes again, fighting off the drowsiness that threatened to engulf him. He passed a hand over his face and sought for words with which to make his report.

" The Sioux, sir !" he croaked.

" Take it easy, son. What about the Sioux?" Custer's voice was gentle, kindly, but there was a note of impatience, of controlled excitement in it.

Jim reached for the brandy glass the commanding officer held out again. He took another sip, and felt himself gaining strength, and collecting his thoughts.

" Sitting Bull is making trouble, sir," he started. " We saw him address a big council. Sergeant O'Keefe heard every word . . ."

On and on he went, the words tumbling out of his mouth as Patrick's phrases came back to him. He wasn't content to give the bare message, and Custer listened intently as the weary boy described their encounter with the Medicine Chief of the Sioux, of the hunting parties they had seen and spied upon, and the reaction of the braves to Sitting Bull's words.

"You've done well, Peters—very well," said Custer as Jim fell silent, his story told. "Now it's time you got some sleep. You're excused duty for twenty-four hours. I'll see that Captain Keogh is informed."

It was only then that Jim remembered Comanche.

"My horse!" he gasped, springing to his feet. "I must take care of my horse!"

Colonel Custer smiled. "That's all right, Peters," he said, admiring the concern the young bugler showed for the animal who had served him so well. "The lieutenant will have put an orderly on to it by now. You just go to your quarters and catch up on your sleep. Dismiss."

"Yessir."

A moment or two later Jim Peters walked stiffly across the parade ground, towards "I" company barrack room and the warmth and comfort of his bunk. But the thought of Comanche being cared for by other, strange hands annoyed him. It just didn't seem right. Captain Keogh had insisted that he took care of Comanche—and to Jim's mind that meant from the moment he rode out of the fort, until the moment he reported to the company commander with his horse safe and sound, and none the worse for his punishing ride.

So it was that Jim retraced his steps, making for the company stables, just as Colonel Custer stepped out on to the porch of his quarters to smoke a final pipe, while he considered all that he had learned from Patrick O'Keefe's report.

"Now what in the name of Thunder is that bugler doing?" he asked himself as he saw Jim change his course and turn his back on the barrack room and the bed to which he had been ordered.

Custer watched idly, thinking that perhaps the duty

officer had hailed him or that a patrolling guard commander had challenged him. He saw Jim disappear from sight, swallowed up in the dense shadows of a store shed. He waited for a minute or two, expecting to hear voices—but nothing came to him.

"That's strange," the commander muttered. "What's that young varmint up to?"

Curiosity got the better of Lt.-Colonel George Armstrong Custer. He slipped his pipe into his tunic pocket and strolled across to find out for himself what had happened to Jim Peters. He had barely gone twenty yards when a light sprang into being in the window set in the end wall of " I " company stables. He quickened his pace.

The top half of the stable door was open when the colonel reached it. Light flooded down from a lantern, illuminating the shiny backs and hindquarters of some thirty horses. A slight figure held the lantern high as he passed down the length of the stable, examining every horse. He came to a halt before a large well-proportioned bay gelding.

Colonel Custer heard the horse give a gentle whinny of recognition and saw Jim Peters raise the lantern higher while he made a thorough check of its condition.

"You'll do, old feller," Custer heard his bugler tell the horse. "That orderly sure did know his job. See you in the mornin', Comanche."

Next moment the light was doused, and Jim, content now that he had found out for himself how his horse had fared, slung the lantern back where he had found it, and made for the door.

For a fleeting second the Colonel toyed with the idea of revealing himself, and slating the youngster for disobeying orders. Discipline was discipline after all, and had to be maintained constantly, without let-up. But something checked the commander of the Seventh

Cavalry. He stepped back into the shadows and watched as Jim bolted and barred the door, after taking one last look at where Comanche, groomed, and watered, munched happily at a double ration of well-earned oats. There were times when discipline took second place to a cavalryman's concern for his horse—and this was one of those times.

Totally unaware of the tall, ram-rod backed figure who stood in the shadows, Jim Peters dragged his weary body off to bed—content at last. Behind him, Colonel Custer chuckled quietly to himself, making a mental note which was to have far-reaching effects upon the future of Bugler Jim Peters of the Seventh before many months were out.

CHAPTER FOURTEEN

ULTIMATUM

THE WHOLE of the Fort Abraham Lincoln barracks was buzzing with rumour and conjecture. The news of the return of a courier late at night, and the fact that the Colonel had seen fit to admit him to his personal quarters, was enough to start the know-alls and the wiseacres off in no mean fashion.

When it was learned that the commanding officer had left by train for Washington, the rumours knew no bounds at all. Jim was pestered night and day by his fellow members of " I " company to divulge what his message had contained, and what the effect upon the men of the Seventh was likely to be. He held his peace, refusing to say a word, and he was more than glad when Patrick O'Keefe and the other members of the scouting party returned. The Irish sergeant made short work of the rumour-mongers, warning them that they would be disciplined if they persisted in their gossip.

To Jim the next few days were a complete anti-climax to his hectic ride and the rigours of the scouting patrol. He had expected immediate action to forestall Sitting Bull. He had pictured Colonel Custer leading a detachment of the Seventh out at the double to order the Sioux back to the Reservation, and to demonstrate the formidable might of the American Army. Instead, the commander had disappeared, the dark-eyed, conceited Major Marcus Reno had taken over command, and life continued as before.

Jim couldn't understand it. He sought out Patrick O'Keefe.

"Anyone would think our report wasn't of any importance," he complained. "What goes on, Patrick?"

The Irish sergeant smiled. "Ye've got a lot to learn about the Army," he said sadly.

"What d'you mean?" Jim bristled at the rebuke.

"Custer's only a lieutenant-colonel, don't forget," Patrick explained. "He has to take orders from full colonels, an' brigadiers, an' generals o' all kinds. He can't make a move without permission from General Terry, an' in a case like this the whole question of action against the Sioux may well have to go before the Secretary for War—or even the President."

"But that might take weeks!" Jim gasped.

"Yes, it might easily. That's why it was so urgent to get back with the news, lad. Otherwise it may have taken even longer to convince the top brass o' the urgency o' the situation, an' by the time they got around to issuin' orders the winter would have been upon us. Ye can't hurry generals or politicians. Custer was the only general I ever came across who acted first an' worried about the consequences afterwards. He could get away with it *then*, but he's only a lieutenant-colonel now—not a major-general."

"How long will they take to make up their minds?" Jim asked, sadly disillusioned by the whole business.

"Two—three weeks, I figure," said Patrick. "If Custer's luck holds."

But Colonel Custer's luck didn't hold.

The commander of the Seventh Cavalry returned from Washington several weeks later—in a flaming temper. The matter of the Sioux and Sitting Bull's intentions had been taken out of his hands entirely. It had become a political issue, requiring the authority of the Secretary for War and President Grant himself before any troops or even envoys could take the field.

For days the irate commander didn't trust himself to

leave his quarters. He strode up and down, hour after hour, like a caged lion—cursing the stupidity of politicians in a voice that could be heard halfway into Bismark.

"He's really got his hair off this time," chuckled Trooper Siggers as he went off duty after mounting guard close to Custer's quarters. "Heaven help us when he decides to get back to work with the training o' the Seventh. He'll drill us mornin' noon an' night."

Sure enough, when Colonel Custer did appear, he drove his troops without let-up, ordering officers and men out on manœuvres at a few hours' notice, rousing the troopers from their bunks in the dead of night for surprise exercises and practice alarms, while he haunted the telegraph shack, in hourly expectation of orders from General Terry.

Day after day went by, and still the telegraph was silent. Custer's rage smouldered deep within him, turning him from a dashing, dare-devil commander into a snarling, bitter martinet.

The troopers of the Seventh suffered the Colonel's moods and temperaments with surprisingly good grace. They moaned and grumbled, admittedly, but they were cavalrymen, and it was easy for them to understand the frustration and bitter resentment the "General" felt towards all superior officers and politicians. After months of endless drills and ceremonials they too were itching to take to the field and do a worth-while job for a change. If their commander chose to take it out on them, it was just too bad—someone had to suffer, and their shoulders were broad enough to take anything the "General" could hand out. They loved the man, they sympathised with him—and they were behind him to a man.

It was the officers of the Seventh who resented their Colonel's attitude. Major Reno and Captain Benteen, in particular, bustled about with scowling faces, snapping their acknowledgments of Custer's orders in his face, venting their spite on their juniors, and making life unbearable for all around them. First Lieutenant Cooke, the Colonel's adjutant, grew more and more morose as he relayed the harsh, overbearing instructions from Custer to his officers. It seemed that the commander picked upon the slightest slip or oversight, ranting and raving at whoever was responsible—whether he was a trooper, a non-com, or a major with twenty-five years' service. The sullen adjutant had the unenviable task of passing on the Colonel's rebukes, left and right, day in day out.

Of the officers attached to Fort Abraham Lincoln only Captain Keogh remained unchanged by the almost mutinous atmosphere that surrounded him in the officers' mess. He went about his duties with the same unsmiling countenance that was normal to him. He was never seen to show by as much as a flicker of his eye-lashes that he had private feelings or thoughts about the way the commander was driving his regiment.

Captain Keogh was a soldier, through and through. It was his job to take orders and to give orders. He did just that, bottling up his thoughts and feelings with rigid self-discipline.

But the first-sergeants, sergeants and corporals were not built like Captain Keogh. Their prime concern was with the welfare of the men, and the horses they rode. If they felt their companies or troops were being driven too hard, they vented their wrath in the safety and security of the sergeants' mess—where no officer was allowed to enter without permission from themselves.

"If 'Yellowhair' goes on like this much longer," said Sergeant Schultz one night when "I" company had returned from a two-day manœuvre with their horses in terrible shape, and themselves not much better, " I'll begin to feel like Major Reno—though heaven knows I don't like the little turkey cock. My boys are being drilled off their feet. They're goin' stale. At this rate they won't be fit for action if or when it comes."

Patrick O'Keefe nodded his agreement. " Ye're right, Schultz," he sighed. " Much as I admire Custer, I can't see what's got into him. He must learn to control himself if he's to retain the respect o' the men. They'll take just so much—then they'll crack. Much more o' this and the ' General ' will have a mutiny on his hands."

It was late October now, with the temperature dropping fast, and the river fogs settling over the Missouri in a thick blanket of white. Winter was just around the corner. Scouts still slipped out of the fort at regular intervals—keeping Custer informed of the progress of Sitting Bull's mission to the buffalo hunters. Their news was bad. More and more Indians were leaving the Reservation on the pretext of a final hunt before winter settled in with a vengeance, and those who were already out had made permanent camps near the Yellowstone and Powder rivers and were obviously intending to stay there indefinitely.

As more and more reports came in, and the weather grew progressively worse, Colonel Custer shook himself out of his black mood of frustration. There was no use in shouting against thunder. It was now too late to avert the fighting that Sitting Bull's action had made inevitable. He had done what he could, and Washington had seen fit to dilly and dally senselessly. He washed his hands of the whole affair. " Let General Terry sort it out from here," he thought with bitter resignation.

Colonel Custer relaxed, his anger still smouldering, but now well under control. The Seventh Cavalry, from bugler boy to second-in-command, let out a heartfelt sigh of relief, and began their preparations for a winter which promised to be as bitter as any they had experienced.

The first snows were starting, howling from the northwest on the biting wind, when the telegraph key began to jump in the shack across the parade ground, by the main barrack block.

Minutes later telegraph-corporal Feekins flung open the door, and bellowed for an orderly. No one answered. The duty orderlies were huddled round the redhot stove in the guardhouse, deaf to all shouting noncoms, and concerned only with spinning out in comfort the half-hour left before mess call.

Heaping curses upon the heads of all orderlies, and all privates first or second class, Corporal Feekins stepped out into the teeth of the falling snow, and began to move at a staggering trot towards the Colonel's quarters.

It was December 3rd 1875. The telegraph message in Corporal Feekins' hand read thus:

To Lt.-Colonel Custer, commanding 7th U.S. Cavalry, Fort Abraham Lincoln, North Dakota, U.S.A.

By order of the Secretary for War, envoys have gone to all principal chiefs of the Sioux Nation instructing them and their people that unless they shall remove within the bounds of their Reservation (and remain there) before the 31st January next, they shall be deemed hostile and treated accordingly by the military force.

You will receive detailed orders by further telegraph.
Signed. *Alfred H. Terry, General,*
Commanding Officer, Department of Dakota.

The Government had at last made up its mind—just three months too late!

Every man in the Seventh Cavalry now knew that it was only a matter of time before they would take the field in a large-scale operation to drive the Sioux back to the Black Hills.

Sitting Bull had done his work well. Already a thousand Sioux, and several hundred Northern Cheyennes were camped on the plains, refusing to budge for anyone. The Government order had been the last straw needed to unite the tribes in flagrant defiance of the White Eyes and their Pony Soldiers.

As the deadline of the last day of January drew ever nearer, the troopers and their officers argued nightly over what the future held.

Would Sitting Bull make a real fight of it, or would he give ground and retreat before the threat of the heavily-armed, well-supplied troops?

Would General Terry order an all-out attack by the cavalry regiments under his control combined with the regiments of foot soldiers and artillery companies which were on call at other forts and barracks; or would he leave Custer to make the first move with his crack regiment of horse soldiers?

No one knew—not even Custer. Until the deadline had been reached the lines the action would take were anybody's guess.

January dragged to a close to find Fort Abraham Lincoln in the grip of a raging blizzard. Snow pelted down over the iced-up waters of the Missouri, bringing work to a standstill, and all thought of an Indian campaign right out of the question. Again the men of the Seventh found themselves frustrated. They kicked their heels uselessly about their barracks.

With the dawning of February 1st 1876 the Army

*was at war with the defiant Sioux. All men, women and
children of the Sioux Nation not back on the Reservation had become hostiles.*

The telegraph keys began to tap again—and General
Terry's orders came to the Seventh.

It was to be a full scale operation. The Sioux were to
be taught a final lesson. Three armies were to take the
field with the coming of spring, under the command of
Generals Terry, Gibbon, and Crook, and supplied by a
river steamboat which was to cruise up the Missouri
and enter the Yellowstone. They were to box the Sioux
in towards the Big Horn Mountains and hammer them
until they surrendered. *The Seventh Cavalry was to
form the spearhead of the attack!*

The morale of the men had never been higher. The
Seventh had been recognised as the crack regiment of
the plains country. They had been given pride of place
over all the others. From Colonel Custer downwards
they positively strutted as they made their preparations!

"What did I tell ye, lad?" asked Patrick O'Keefe
with pride when he heard the news. "Any regiment
Custer commands is *bound* to be the crack regiment!
The 'General' will be in his element. When Sittin'
Bull hears that 'Yellowhair' is ridin' at the head o' the
Seventh he'll skedaddle for the Black Hills just as fast
as his moccasins will carry him!"

And then the bombshell dropped.

Colonel Custer was recalled to Washington. He was
ordered to testify as a witness before a Congressional
Committee concerning irregularities in the buying of
stores for the Army. He was relieved of his command
almost on the eve of the campaign!

"That's what comes o' mixin' with politicians,"
snarled Patrick O'Keefe with unusual savagery. "Custer never could keep his mouth shut if he saw dirty
work in Washington, an' now the sly little political

busy-bodies will do their best to break him. We'll be lucky if we ever see 'The General' back here again, Jim."

"Oh, no!" Jim protested, horrified at the idea. "It's not as serious as that, is it?"

"Worse," said Patrick with infinite sadness. "If they don't break his career, they'll do their best to break his heart. From what I've heard the durned fool has been criticisin' a personal friend o' the President!"

"Gee! That's just asking for trouble," gasped Jim Peters.

"Ye can say *that* again, lad," said the unhappy Irishman.

CHAPTER FIFTEEN

SPRING CAMPAIGN

DEPRIVED OF their commander, the hero-worshipping troopers of the Seventh felt their spirits sink to the depths.

Custer was more than just their leader. He was a symbol of all the Cavalry stood for, and what made them feared and respected on the frontier. It was Custer who had taken them from all corners of the States and welded them together by the fire of his enthusiasm until the Seventh was a name to be reckoned with in any council of war. Without him they felt lost. They missed the fantastically high standards of efficiency and bearing on which he insisted. They missed the verve and dash he displayed whenever he swung up into the saddle of his Kentucky thoroughbred to lead them on parade, or on field manœuvres. They missed his unpredictable moods which had them keyed up and anxious to please—and above all they missed him as a man; a swashbuckling, handsome, dare-devil showman who knew more about handling men than a dozen Major Marcus Renos ever would.

Jim Peters felt the loss of Custer as much or more than most of his friends and fellow troopers in " I " company. It was Custer who had taken him into the regiment when he was under age, and it was the commander himself who had selected him from among the eight hundred men at his command to act as his special courier. He felt as though he had lost a personal friend who had his interests at heart.

But whatever the troopers felt or thought, the preparations for the spring campaign continued. General Terry arrived in person to assemble his men and organise the details of the three-pronged attack.

Jim Peters found himself rushed off his feet, dashing here and there with messages from the Adjutant of the Seventh to the various company commanders; obtaining reports of progress from the fatigue parties who checked guns and stores, and from the farriers who worked long hours checking the horses for the long journey ahead.

Fort Abraham Lincoln was fairly busting at the seams with the addition of foot soldiers and supplies. Two companies of the Seventeenth United States Infantry arrived and were crowded into the fort. One company of the Sixth United States Infantry followed, and a pack train of mules was assembled for use as an ammunition column.

Everywhere was bustle and excitement, and for a while the loss of Colonel Custer was pushed to the back of the trooper's minds. General Terry was a fine soldier and a friend of Custer's. The men respected him, and knew that if anything could be done to get the colonel back from Washington in time, he would do it.

"When do you reckon we will start?" Jim asked Patrick O'Keefe as "I" company took a brief break from its labours one bright frosty morning in late February.

"Not until May at the earliest, Jim," the Irish sergeant told him. "There's an almighty lot o' plannin' an' organisin' to do yet. This is the biggest operation for years. It takes a mighty lot o' men to round up several hundred free-roamin' Injuns an' steer 'em back to the Hills. Besides, the supply boats can't get up to us until the river ice breaks."

"So there may be a chance of Colonel Custer getting back here in time?" Jim asked eagerly.

Several other troopers pricked up their ears to hear

Patrick's answer. News of the "General" was always welcome.

"It's doubtful," the sergeant said sadly. "Corporal Feekins told me this mornin' that a telegraph message had come through to say that Custer was in real trouble. He has been reprimanded for being indiscreet about Army matters an' is now awaitin' orders from the Secretary for War. It's like I said, lad; he's been a durned fool an' he's in disgrace."

"It's a cryin' shame!" one of the veterans burst out at Patrick's words. "All he did was write a letter to the papers back in the east sayin' that the men who buy stores for the Army are a lot of rogues, and are gettin' fat on vast profits at the country's expense. We all know it's true—the War Department is rotten with corruption, from top to bottom."

"It's true all right," Patrick O'Keefe agreed. "But a soldier's job is to soldier—not to play at politics. I don't know what came over Custer to do it. It was madness."

"He's always been a law unto himself," chuckled a grizzled veteran. "You'll never be able to keep the 'General' quiet once he gets the bit between his teeth. What's more I'll lay you ten dollars to a cent that he gets away with it. Custer won't miss this campaign—if he has to go down on his knees before the President himself and beg him to post him back to the Seventh."

Trooper Larkin looked up with a sneer. "I'll take that bet, soldier," he said eagerly. "My money says Custer's finished. We shan't see him again as commander of the Seventh."

Corporal Feekins had never been so busy in his life. "Seems every pip-squeak officer in the whole durned Army wants to send love an' kisses to General Terry," he complained bitterly to Sergeant Schultz one morning.

" The blessed wires have been full of hot air for months now. Yap yap yap, mornin', noon an' night."

" What about?"

" Orders an' reports. Seems these pesky officers can't lift their right hand to blow their own noses without askin' permission o' General Terry. First it's General Crook reporting he's havin' trouble roundin' up mules at Fort Fetterman. Then it's General Gibbon complainin' that it's takin' longer than he expected to raise the infantry soldiers from Fort Shaw an' the cavalry from Fort Ellis. If you ask me, Sarge, they're all in a very dickens of a muddle."

Sergeant Schultz laughed. " Just like you, Corporal," he said drily—and ducked out of the telegraph shed before the corporal could throw his pad at him.

In fact, things were going reasonably smoothly. Terry handled his fellow-generals with a tact and wisdom that was rare in any army. Soon the three armies felt the firmness of his grip upon the over-all plan of the campaign. They kicked against it, testing the quality of the leadership, as would a lively horse with a new rider on its back. They received the answering tug of the rein and the bite of the curb, struggled once more in protest—and then settled down to work as a team. From that moment on General Alfred H. Terry knew that he was fully in command.

All that remained now was for the ice to break. The " Far West," a twin-funnelled, two-decked river steamboat under the command of Captain Marsh, was waiting downstream for the first sign of the thaw to start. As soon as it did, the " Far West " would come snorting and puffing up the Missouri to take on stores and equipment, and hustle them up to a depot on the banks of the Yellowstone for later use in supplying the three converging armies.

Day after day went by, and still the ice held—and still no news of Custer came to the Seventh.

Then, suddenly, without the slightest suggestion of warning, the mercury in the thermometer outside the guardhouse soared upwards, the sun shone down out of a cloudless sky, and the gutters overflowed with melting snow water.

The thaw had begun.

Exercising Comanche for Captain Keogh, Jim rode out through the slush and mud of the riverside trail and watched the great chunks of pack ice being torn free as the angry, swollen waters of the Missouri surged underneath the foot-thick covering that had hidden them for four long months.

" Won't be long now, old feller," he remarked to the bay as he leaned forward in the heavy McClellan saddle and stroked Comanche's neck to calm him.

Comanche stirred restlessly, starting every time the ice split apart with a rending crack and bucked and junketed about as it began to break its way out of the mounting mass of floes. The fresh tingling smell of spring was already in the air, and the rangy gelding had been cooped up for too long. He was dying to get the bit between his teeth and show Jim just what he could do in a turn of speed out on the free wild prairie.

The same restlessness was coursing through Jim's veins. He was itching to get into action, to take part in his first campaign. He felt he owed it to his Uncle Moses to play some part in preventing the Sioux from ever bringing death and destruction to the plains and the hills again. He wanted more than anything to be one of the select band of professional soldiers who were prepared to fight to maintain peace on the frontier by all the strength at their command—and he wanted to prove that he could acquit himself with courage when the time came to face the Indians who had been responsible for his uncle's murder.

"Time we got back." He spoke aloud to Comanche, guiding him round with a gentle knee pressure and heading him back towards the fort.

Comanche pranced, skittishly, resenting being made to return within the walls of the fort before he was good and ready. But just as General Terry had curbed his fellow-generals and proved his leadership, so did Jim Peters demonstrate that he was master too, tightening his grip on the reins and letting Comanche know that he would take no nonsense. Just like the generals, the bay gelding tried one last flourish of his proud head, and then fell to trotting calmly and daintily through the oozing mud of the trail back to camp. They understood each other well, those two. They were a team.

Jim never passed under the high archway of the main gate to Fort Abraham Lincoln without a surge of pride in being a member of the famous Seventh. Those glittering brass figures over the gate were the same as the crossed sabres design on his collar. He didn't need reminding that he was a member of the finest regiment in the U.S. Army, but he couldn't help squaring his shoulders just a shade more, and sitting just a little straighter in the saddle. Mounted on Comanche, he wouldn't trade his place or his career with anyone in the whole wide world.

Preoccupied with these thoughts Jim didn't notice the little corporal who ran across the parade ground, nor did he see the officer who appeared around the corner of the barrack building, mounted on a big black Arab horse.

The first Jim Peters knew of Corporal Feekins' disgrace was when the voice of Major Marcus Reno cut across the air with the viciousness of a bull-whacker's whip.

" Corporal! What in blue blazes do you think you're doing?"

Jim looked round with a start, as did every man jack on guard duty or fatigue within a radius of three hundred yards. They saw telegraph-corporal Feekins come to a sliding halt, salute—and then begin to flap a paper up and down before the major's eyes.

" *He's coming back sir! He's coming back!*"

Corporal Feekins was practically dancing with excitement, all discipline forgotten in the wonder of being first with the news.

" *Custer's comin' back, major!*" he shouted joyously.

" *What?*" Major Reno managed to get out just that one astonished word before his horse reared high in fright at the flapping paper and the shouting corporal who all but danced a jig in front of him. The black shied sideways, twisting awkwardly—and Major Marcus A. Reno, acting commander, Seventh U.S. Cavalry, Fort Abraham Lincoln, North Dakota, sailed smartly through the air to land at the startled corporal's feet on the seat of his amply padded uniform breeches.

" Oh golly! Are you all right, Major?" asked Corporal Feekins anxiously as he rushed to help the commander to his feet.

Major Reno simply sat there in the melting snow, resisting all attempts to get him to his feet. His face was dark, empurpled with rage. " *Sergeant!*" he roared to Patrick O'Keefe who had hurried forward to catch his frightened horse.

" Sorr?"

" Arrest that man!"

" Yes, sorr. What charge, sorr?" asked Patrick, doing his best to control the laughter that was bubbling up inside him.

Major Reno staggered to his feet. " Insubordination.

Conduct unbecoming a non-commissioned officer. And
. . . and . . ."

" . . . gross disrespect to the *actin'* commander?" suggested Patrick innocently.

Major Reno stuck his head forward and glared at the
Irishman as though he wanted to strangle him. " I'll
remember that, Sergeant!" he snarled. " Get back to
your duties!"

" Yess, sorr!"

As Patrick O'Keefe turned away, Jim saw Major
Reno snatch the telegraph form from Corporal Feekins'
hands. " On second thoughts, Corporal," he said icily
after he had read it, " I feel you are more useful to the
regiment on telegraph duty. You will be confined to
camp for fourteen days."

" Yessir," said the telegraph-corporal with a face as
long as a bloodhound, and Major Reno stalked off to
change his sodden uniform.

Jim Peters hurried up. " Is it true, Corp?" he
demanded.

Feekins grinned. " True as I stand here confined to
camp," he chuckled happily. " Custer's due back any
day."

" Gee!" said Jim Peters. " Now that's really *somethin'*!"

As usual Corporal Feekins exaggerated. It was
several days before Lt.-Colonel Custer rode into Fort
Abraham Lincoln to take his rightful place at the head
of his regiment. By the time he arrived the " Far West "
had nosed up from Yankton, tied up at the jetty and
loaded her stores. All was now set for the word from
General Terry to put the army into the field.

Custer came back like a whirlwind. The officers and
men of the Seventh had thought themselves driven hard
before, but now they realised with a shock that the

"General" could work them even harder. By May 10th all was ready—horses, mules, stores, ammunition and men. On the following day the Seventh moved out of Fort Abraham Lincoln in formal order, headed by the full band of the regiment. That night they slept far out on the prairie, under canvas.

The spring campaign had begun.

CHAPTER SIXTEEN

CHANGE OF PLAN

" Peters !"

" Sir."

Jim Peters stepped smartly forward from the ranks of " I " company drawn up for inspection in the cold greyness of the dawn.

" You are to report to First Lieutenant Cooke at Regimental headquarters, immediately," said Captain Keogh. " As from now you will act under his orders."

" Yessir."

Wondering what was expected of him, Jim hurried to the Adjutant's tent in the centre of the canvas town, beside the commanding officer's quarters.

Lt. Cooke, morose and sullen as usual, greeted him with tired, red-rimmed eyes. He had been up half the night with Colonel Custer, taking notes, writing orders for the company commanders, and dealing with the mass of field reports and forms which were the curse of all staff officers and adjutants. He didn't keep Jim waiting long.

" Peters, you are to act as special orderly to myself and the Colonel," he stated brusquely. " You are relieved of all company duties and will remain within call twenty-four hours a day. Understand?"

" Yessir !"

Jim was delighted. It meant constant hard work with little chance of relaxation, but it was worth it. He would be at the hub of the whole regiment—in touch with all that went on. *Personal orderly to the Colonel!* It was a distinct feather in his cap. What was more, when he left the tent he found Patrick O'Keefe had been attached to the Colonel's staff as well. Things were working out very nicely!

Patrick greeted him warmly. " Ye've done well, lad," he grinned. " I was there when the ' General ' asked for ye by name. Ye've certainly made yer mark with him. Keep it up an' ye will earn yer stripes one day."

Jim beamed with pleasure. Asked for by Colonel Custer in person! He felt very proud.

" What are *your* duties, Patrick?" he asked.

" I'm in charge o' the scouts," the sergeant explained. " Custer's got several Crow Indians an' a few Rees as well for trackin'. They are fannin' out ahead o' us all the time with orders to report back the minute they strike fresh signs o' the Sioux."

" Indians?" Jim jerked out in surprise. " Can we trust them?"

Patrick O'Keefe put back his head and roared with laughter. " Trust them?" he echoed. " I'll say we can! The Crows an' the Rees are deadly enemies o' the Sioux an' the Cheyennes. They have been for generations. They're only happy when they have fresh Sioux scalps hangin' on their bridles!"

Jim was to meet the Indian scouts sooner than he expected. They rode in an hour later, just as he was returning from taking a message to Captain Benteen for the Adjutant.

" Any luck, boys?" demanded Patrick as the blanketed braves joined the column, which was now in full motion—its tents and gear stacked in the lumbering supply wagons that took up the rear of the troops. Bloody Knife—Custer's favourite scout—shrugged. " It is early yet," he grunted. " We have many streams and rivers to cross, and many miles to travel before we reach the buffalo plains of the Sioux dogs. But we shall find them before many days, my friend." His eyes flashed happily at the thought. " Then there will be much slaughter," he added.

Jim Peters shuddered at the words, reading the cruel lines of the Crow scout's sneering lips.

" I shouldn't want to have him on *my* tail," he muttered to Patrick as the four Indians, Bloody Knife, Curly, White-Man-Runs-Him, and Hairy Moccasin, rode off to report to Custer.

" Nor me," said Patrick, wrinkling his nose with distaste. " Never did like mixin' with Crows. They stink worse than a bull buffalo in a stagnant mud hole !"

But whatever their characters, or their unsavoury personal odours, the Crow scouts certainly knew their job. Jim Peters found himself ordered out to join them ahead of the slow-moving column on several occasions in the next few days with instructions to return at once with news of any contact with hostiles. He saw them reading tracks in the soft spring turf of the prairie lands with such skill that they could tell the exact day on which they had been made, by whom, and the speed at which they had been travelling. He even became friendly with Curly and Hairy Moccasin, getting them to teach him to read signs, and to explain what they looked for as they scanned the terrain ahead.

Curly was a born teacher. With infinite patience he taught Jim to recognise one set of pony tracks from another, until the young bugler could tell the size and height of the animal by the shape and depth of its print. He taught him how it could be told whether the rider had been a brave or a squaw, or whether the unshod pony had been travelling fast or slow. He pointed out signs which Jim would never have noticed in a month if he hadn't been shown.

" Papoose in this party," Curly said one day, pointing to an empty puff ball lying beside the trail.

"How d'you know?" Jim demanded.

Curly grinned. "Squaw use dust of puff ball for papoose's skin!" he chuckled. "Moss and dust keep Indian papoose clean."

But all the sign they found was old sign—made weeks before. Of the main party of the Sioux there was no indication at all.

The long column of cavalry and the following foot soldiers and supply waggons would on across the plains day after day, drawing closer and closer to the Big Horn Mountains. Custer, irritable and impatient of every delay, rode at the head of the column with two troops of cavalry as an advance guard. Major Reno took the right wing with companies B, C, I, E, F, and L, led by Captains Keogh and Yates. Captain Benteen rode to the left commanding the six remaining companies of the regiment with the help of Captains Weir and French. Each commander split his troopers into three —advance guard, flank guard, and rear guard—protecting the slow-moving infantry who formed the main body of the column.

Immediately behind Colonel Custer's spearhead rode General Terry and his staff, at the head of a full company of foot soldiers. Then came a battalion of Gatling guns, a second company of infantry, and the waggons, four abreast. A final company of foot soldiers took up the rear. It was a heavy unwieldy column, stretching for the best part of a mile and a half and travelling at a speed which rarely exceeded ten to fourteen miles in a full day.

Jim smiled to himself as he saw the heavily-laden troopers of his old company jogging along in all weathers, weighed down with spare equipment and ammunition. *His* kit was safely loaded into the head-quarters waggon, leaving him free to move fast at a minute's notice. "I" company horses, like all the others, had eighty or ninety pounds of equipment to carry in addition to a hundred rounds of ammunition and the weight of their riders.

By the 19th the column had reached the Sweet Briar River, found it in flood and detoured far to the south. They made camp at Turkey Buzzard Roost, without wood for cooking fires, then pressed on through pouring rain and showers of sleet, and on the 22nd May reached gaunt hills of alkali rock, covered with scrub, cactus and sagebrush. They made camp that night on Thin Woman Creek.

On the 23rd Jim was ordered to ride ahead with Curly and Bloody Knife once again.

They had ridden barely ten miles when Curly pointed to the dome of a nearby hill. "Sioux," he grunted.

Three braves, mounted on pinto ponies, were visible on the skyline for a second or two before they wheeled away and disappeared from sight. They were the first hostiles to be sighted in a fortnight's hard travel. Jim rode back at once, spurring to reach Colonel Custer with the least delay.

But though the column spread out, and wave after wave of troopers combed the country on all sides, they saw not a suspicion of hostile Indians again. They had flushed a lone hunting party, and were no nearer the main body of Sitting Bull's defiant tribesmen than they had been before.

General Terry was becoming more and more restless, and Custer was eating out his heart at the delay.

"Where in Hades are they?" Jim heard the colonel rage that night through the thin walls of his tent. "A mass of hostiles like Sitting Bull's got can't just hide themselves away!"

But General Terry had further worries. His whole

plan had depended upon finding the hostiles long before this. If they didn't make contact with the Sioux in the next few days he would have to alter the entire timing of the other columns. General Crook was advancing northwards with eight hundred men, General Gibbon was moving in from the west with nearly five hundred, and Terry and Custer between them had the best part of a thousand foot and horse soldiers moving further and further westwards.

On and on the army pushed, with still no sign of the Sioux.

By the evening of June 3rd they reached Beaver Creek and made camp, wet, miserable and worried.

Then, just as tempers were getting frayed and the morale of the troops was dropping hour by hour, a courier was seen to break into the valley and spur hard towards them. Patrick O'Keefe and his scouts rode out at once to intercept him.

The courier proved to be from General Gibbon. He had sighted the Sioux. They were moving freely about the territory due south of the Yellowstone River, flanked by the Big Horn Mountains to the west and the Powder river to the east.

A second courier arrived before the day was out, reporting that the " Far West " was in position at Stanley's Stockade on the Yellowstone and had unloaded her supplies.

Of General Crook and his column there was no news at all.

General Terry didn't hesitate. He scrapped his original plan, and handed over command to Custer. He gave him orders to proceed to the mouth of the Powder river, where it poured its dark and filthy waters into the Yellowstone, and himself sped ahead to contact Captain Marsh of the " Far West " and arrange a meeting with General Gibbon. Captain Keogh and Captain

Moyland rode with him at the head of " I " and " A "
companies, as the General's escort.

Jim Peters felt a pang of jealousy as he saw his own
company ride off, with its guidon flag fluttering bravely.
He would have given his eye teeth to have gone with
them and been one of the first to sight the broad waters
of the Yellowstone.

But he had little time for regret, for Colonel Custer,
exultant now that he had full command, issued a string
of curt commands which kept his Adjutant yelling for
his courier time and time again.

Jim had never been so busy. He sped from company
to company with new orders; from Major Reno to
Captain Benteen, on to the artillery commander, back
to the officer commanding the infantry. He carried
word to the waggoners, to the mule-packers, and the
rearguard. He heard the muttered curses of the various
commanders as they read the " General's " orders, and
saw the dark scowls which broke over the faces of the
fiery Major Reno, and the resentful Captain Benteen.
It was plain that Custer was throwing his weight about,
and his officers didn't like it. After the tact and courtesy of General Terry, Custer's attitude was grossly
unpopular.

Lashed by the " General's " tongue, the whole column
moved off at a smart pace. The waggons closed up,
the infantry struggled manfully to keep pace with the
escorting cavalry, and the Gatling gun company
whipped their horses into action, urging them forward
over the rock and mud of the churned-up trail at a
pace that threatened to shift the guns from their mount-
ings.

The troopers of the Seventh chuckled to themselves as
they heard the muttered curses which were piled upon
Custer's head by their officers.

" Do 'em good! " grinned a grizzled trooper in Reno's

command. "They need a bit o' shakin' up now an' again, an' the "General" is just the boy to do it!"

But when Jim Peters eventually went off duty that night after the heaviest day's mileage of the whole journey, he found Patrick O'Keefe gazing thoughtfully into the bottom of his coffee mug as he sat before a carefully nursed fire and dried his steaming clothes.

"What's on your mind, Patrick?" he asked as he sank down beside the sergeant and helped himself to coffee.

Patrick O'Keefe looked up with a start.

"Oh, it's ye, Jim!" he said. "I was just thinkin' that I don't like it at all."

"You don't like what?"

"The way Custer's buildin' up trouble for himself, lad."

"How d'you mean?"

Patrick O'Keefe shrugged, tugging at his moustache with one hand as he sought the words with which to express himself.

"He's ridin' the regiment with a tight curb, an' spurrin' it at the same time," he stated sadly. "That's no way to act. It would spoil any quality horse, and it'll spoil a quality regiment if he's not careful. An army wants leadin', not drivin'. If he slams his officers much more he'll have them workin' against him, instead o' with him, as a team. It's team work that wins battles. Teamwork an' the loyalty o' men an' officers."

"You're tired, Patrick," said Jim. "We're all tired an' jumpy. The 'General' will calm down in the morning."

But Patrick O'Keefe shook his head. "No, son, he won't," he answered with conviction. "Custer's not the man he was, by a long chalk. He's still smartin' at his disgrace in Washington. He's eatin' out his heart to get into action an' prove himself as the dare-devil cavalry leader he used to be. He wants glory—personal glory, an' he doesn't care how he gets it any more. He's headin' us for trouble."

"What, from the Sioux?" Jim asked.

"No," came the firm, considered answer. "From Major Marcus A. Reno."

CHAPTER SEVENTEEN

STRIP FOR ACTION!

BY now it was clear to everyone in the command that the Sioux were somewhere in the area of the Tongue River and Rosebud Creek. This was confirmed by General Gibbon when he came down river to meet General Terry at the mouth of the Powder River.

"They're somewhere between the two rivers," Gibbon had said. "We sighted the first Sioux from the north bank of the Yellowstone, but they moved out of sight and we couldn't follow. They were south of the river and we were north."

"How many?" General Terry had asked.

"Can't say. We only saw one village—on the move after buffalo."

Within an hour of arrival at the mouth of the Powder River, Custer's command learned this report, to a man, in the mysterious way that all soldiers managed to find out what their commanders were discussing. An orderly overheard a chance phrase as he went about his duties; a scout put two and two together from a second chance remark; a corporal pieced both to make a certain whole; and from his mouth the news sped through the regimental streets of tents and bivouacs. That was the way of a campaigning Army. That was the "grapevine" news service of the serving soldier.

"I'm lost," admitted Jim Peters when he heard the news. "I'm all mixed up with the Yellowstone, the Powder, the Tongue, the Rosebud—and what was that other river, Patrick?"

The sergeant grinned. "The Little Big Horn," he said. "It's simple really, Jim. I'll draw ye a map."

Jim bent forward eagerly as Patrick O'Keefe traced a rough map of the area in the sand of the river bank. With one slash of the shining steel tip of his sabre he drew a line due east and west. "That's the Yellowstone," he announced. "It flows from the west to the east, where it empties into the upper reaches o' the Missouri, above Fort Lincoln."

"I've got that," Jim told him with impatience. "But where are the other rivers?"

Patrick ignored him. "The Yellowstone has a lot o' tributaries," he continued. "They rise in the Montana highlands in the south. They run due north, parallel with each other until they meet the Yellowstone at right angles."

"But which is which?" Jim asked.

"Running from east to west ye come to the Powder River first. That's where we are now—where it joins the Yellowstone. Then further west ye meet the Tongue River. Further west lies Rosebud Creek; an' beyond that yet come to the Big Horn an' the Little Big Horn, an' at the edge o' the basin the Big Horn mountains rise up in a north-south ridge. Got it?"

"Yes, thanks," said Jim as he stared at the lines drawn in the sand and committed the plan to his memory. "That simplifies the whole set-up." He wasn't to know then that maps similar to the one Patrick had just drawn were to appear in every newspaper throughout America, and were to be printed in history books all over the con-

tinent. Nor did he ever dream that the area into which
the Seventh Cavalry were moving was to become a
national monument to the struggle for freedom of the
Sioux Nation against the might of the United States
Army.

History was in the making—and Jim Peters, bugler
and special courier to the commander of the Seventh,
was about to become part of it.

On the following morning Jim found himself riding
out from headquarters with orders for Major Reno.

"The Colonel's compliments, sir," he cried as he
sprang from his saddle and saluted.

"Well, what is it? Out with the message, boy!"
Reno snapped irritably.

"The Colonel requests that you report to his tent at
once for a conference with himself and General Terry,
sir," Jim told him, stifling his anger at the major's tone.

"My compliments to *the General*," Reno answered
sulkily. "Tell him I shall be right with him."

"Yessir."

Within an hour Major Marcus Reno rode out of the
Powder River base camp at the head of his six companies. He had orders to scout, with care and secrecy,
the area of the Tongue River, but to go no further west.

General Terry was closing the trap around the Sioux,
stage by stage—river by river. If the Indians weren't
to be found around the Tongue, the army would move
in. Then a further scouting party would scour the Rosebud, while General Cook moved steadily up to block
the southward trails, and General Gibbon moved into
position to block the northern banks of the Yellowstone.
Sitting Bull was about to be boxed in for good.

Major Reno was away nearly ten days, and both
Custer and Terry grew increasingly impatient.

"Where on earth has he got to?" General Terry complained bitterly on the morning of the tenth day.

Custer shrugged. "I wish you had seen fit to send me in person, sir," he said with characteristic bluntness. "Ten to one Reno has exceeded his orders. I don't trust that fellow further than I could kick him!"

"Then you have no right to be in command of the regiment, sir!" thundered Terry, losing his patience and stamping angrily off to his own tent.

That reprimand rankled. Custer was like a bear with a sore head all day.

"God help the Sioux when Custer gets among them!" said several of the troopers.

"If ye ask me it'll be God help us," answered Patrick O'Keefe soberly. "How in blue blazes can Custer fight when he's at loggerheads with his own officers an' with his commandin' general?"

Reno returned that night with his whole command intact. He had news of the greatest importance.

"I scouted the Tongue, sir," he reported to Terry. "There wasn't a sign of a hostile anywhere. But as I was leaving the valley my scouts reported Indian sign towards the Rosebud. I investigated . . ."

"*You what?*" Terry thundered.

"I . . . I . . . I investigated, sir."

"You rode to the Rosebud, against explicit orders?"

Major Reno went two shades paler. "I used my judgment, sir," he said stiffly.

"And what did your precious judgment result in?" Custer sneered.

This time Reno went two shades darker in the face, as he bottled up his rage.

"I came upon a small party of Sioux on the move," he spluttered. "What is more there were many tracks from a very large party right through the area."

"Were you seen?" Terry demanded coldly.

" Y-y-yes, sir. I guess so."

" And with six companies behind you, you didn't attack?" Custer roared.

" My orders said nothing about attacking," Major Reno answered unhappily.

General Terry's icy tones broke in with dreadful clarity. " Your orders were for secrecy at all costs, Major Reno. Having broken those orders and been discovered you should have attacked at once."

" I used my judgment, sir," Reno protested weakly.

" Your *judgment* as you call it has resulted in all elements of surprise being lost," Terry snarled. " You can look forward to facing a court martial at the conclusion of this campaign, Major. Dismiss!"

" Yes, sir," said Reno as he saluted and walked away like a whipped dog.

General Terry turned to Custer, fuming with rage. " It's up to *you* now, Colonel," he barked out. " You will proceed to the Rosebud with the Seventh, trace the Sioux's main village, and get into position to attack. I shall follow as speedily as possible with the infantry and the artillery. Do not attack until I am fully in support —unless action is, in your judgment, utterly vital, and you are certain of success with the limited forces at your command. Do you understand me, Colonel?"

" Perfectly, sir." cried Custer, his eyes sparkling.

" I have full confidence in the quality of *your* judgment," General Terry stressed. " You are the most experienced Indian fighter of us all. But I must emphasize that you are to delay action for as long as possible to give Crook, Gibbon and myself time to get up with you. Remember I have still heard nothing of the whereabouts of General Crook's column, though I have every reason to believe that they are already blocking the southern escape lanes of the Sioux."

" I understand exactly," Custer smiled. " You can

trust me, General. I am also greatly conscious of the honour you do me."

"Carry on then, Colonel," said Terry, with his first smile for days. "And good luck to the Seventh."

Colonel Custer barely paused to thank the General for his good wishes before he was shouting for his orderly.

Jim Peters sprang forward from where his horse was tethered within earshot of all that had happened.

"Sir!" he cried.

"Take my orders to all company commanders of the Seventh," Custer thundered. He paused with the instinct of the true showman that he was, to give the greatest effect to the phrase which followed.

"*They are to strip for action, at once!*"

"Yes, *sir!*" Jim answered as he sprang for his horse.

"Strip for Action" was the order Jim carried to the Seventh, and it was just that that the officers and troopers did, stripping to the bare minimum of stores and equipment. Sabres were discarded, for they were little use against horsemen of the quality of the Sioux, who fought wisely, firing bows and rifles and then wheeling away to circle and fire again. There was no point in carrying a heavy, curved sabre into battle against a foe who never came close enough for a man to strike at him —at any rate that was Custer's theory, and one that was recognised as right in nine cases out of ten; though there were several officers and men who complained at the order. In their view "long knives" were feared by all Indians, and the sight of a cavalry charge coming fast towards them with the sun flashing on the naked steel was enough to strike fear into the bravest Sioux heart. But Custer was adamant; his troops were to travel light, and sabres were to be left behind.

Each man carried one hundred rounds of carbine ammunition for his Springfield, and twenty-four rounds

of revolver ammunition for his Colt or Remington.
This, apart from his immediate personal kit and twelve
pounds of oats for his horse, was the only extra weight
carried. The rest of the ammunition, amounting to
fifty rounds of carbine cartridges per man, was loaded
on to pack mules along with fifteen days' ration of hard
bread, coffee and sugar, and twelve days' ration of bacon.

They rode off to the envious shouts and good wishes
of the infantry, the waggoners and the artillery, with
Custer stiff and formal at their head—his personal flag
fluttering beside him where it was carried by Sergeant
Patrick O'Keefe, and the guidon of the Seventh held
proudly on his other flank by a guidon-corporal. Behind
them rode the adjutant, First Lieutenant Cooke, and the
bearer of the star-spangled banner of the United States.

It was wonderful to be free of the screeching row of
the waggon wheels, the crack of the mule-whackers'
whips, and the slow, plodding pace of the infantry. The
Seventh was entirely by itself from now on, a close-
knit, self-contained unit, with fifteen days' rations, the
prospect of a fight ahead, and no one to give them orders
or slow their progress save their own commander. What
more could a cavalryman want?

It was the 22nd June, 1876. They had travelled nearly
four hundred muscle-aching, man and horse-killing miles
in all weathers from blistering hot sunshine to rainstorms
and sleet. They had been on the trail since the 17th May
and had averaged little more than ten miles a day since
they left Fort Abraham Lincoln on the far Missouri. Now,
the regiment was free of all restriction at last!

To show them what they could do, Custer took the
Seventh over fourteen miles of rough country that first
day between noon and four o'clock, crossing the Rosebud
two miles above its mouth, and heading up the far bank,
due south of the Yellowstone, in Major Reno's tracks.
They camped early that night, bedding down com-

fortably in the dry red soil of the valley. They fed well
too, on small game and fish in addition to their own
rations, and they slept soundly, tired and happy after
their long ride, and with the knowledge that no bugle
calls would waken them—for Custer had ordered such
calls to cease now that they were almost upon the hostiles.

"I don't know why I brought the blessed thing with
me," Jim grumbled as he laid his gleaming instrument
down beside him and crawled into his blankets. "I
haven't blown a note since I left the fort."

Patrick O'Keefe smiled. "Ye'll get plenty o' practice
shortly, lad," he commented quietly. "Ye'll be blowin'
the 'Charge' before many days are out."

"Let's hope I don't have to blow Taps," Jim retorted
—referring to the final call of the day, which was also
played at funerals. The grisly joke brought no comment
from the sergeant. He was already asleep. A moment or
two later Jim Peters fell asleep, too, already regretting
his words and glad that Patrick hadn't heard them.

CHAPTER EIGHTEEN

THE LITTLE BIG HORN VALLEY

FETCHED OUT of their blankets at four o'clock to face
the clammy mist of the river valley, the column of
troopers was on the move, dressed, inspected, break-
fasted and saddled up, before five a.m.

Up and up the Rosebud they moved, taking the criss-
cross trail through the narrow rocky valley beside the
creek. At places the trail grew so narrow that they had
to cross the water and travel up the far bank, where
the going was easier. In all they crossed five or six
times, delayed by the awkward stubbornness of the

pack mules which were causing considerable trouble to Captain Benteen who, poor fellow, had charge of them.

By noon they had covered fifteen miles, and had to halt for the mules to catch up. They pushed on later after a dry and tasteless meal, and had soon covered a further fifteen miles.

Major Reno rode forward from the head of his companies and warned Custer that they were about to reach the limit of his previous scout. It was close to this spot that he had seen the tracks made by a large village of Sioux on the move towards the Little Big Horn River.

They came upon the tracks as the valley widened out and the lush young growth of buffalo grass showed fresh and green on the undulating ground. The turf was scarred in all directions, for some three hundred yards in width across the valley floor. The marks made by several hundred travois poles were jumbled and confused by the hoofprints of many, many unshod ponies. Discarded feathers, pieces of rawhide, and the bones of recently killed buffalo lay in silent evidence of the passage of a large village of Indians.

" Thank heaven they're not all braves in a party that size," said Patrick O'Keefe as he eyed the tracks.

" How d'you mean?" Jim asked.

" Only one in four, on average, of the members of an Indian village are braves or fightin' men," Patrick explained. " The rest are made up o' squaws, maidens, old men an' young boys—not countin' the papooses o' all shapes an' sizes. When ye see a village ye think there's an almighty lot o' opposition—until ye count just the braves. Then ye aren't so worried. Things don't look so bad after all."

Now Custer halted his troops, sending Bloody Knife, Curly and Hairy Moccasin ahead to scout, with a troop of cavalry to help cover the whole area. They returned at nightfall with the news that they had seen not as much as a single hostile, but that the whole country was full of fresh sign. They were certain that a very large village lay within forty miles or so as the crow flies, somewhere along the lower reaches of the Little Big Horn River.

Next morning Jim Peters awoke to find Patrick O'Keefe bending over him, shaking his shoulder.

"On yer feet, lad," the sergeant said. "Ye're detailed to come scoutin' with me."

Dawn was only just breaking when Patrick, Jim, and the two principal scouts, Bloody Knife and Curly, rode out to scour the country to the west.

Jim smiled as he watched the Crow Indians quartering the ground, checking on every little thing in their search for evidence of the recent progress of the Sioux. "They're just like bloodhounds," he grinned to Patrick.

"Better," Patrick grinned back.

Working for the most part in silence, the scouting partly followed every gully, draw and ravine they came across, leaving no cover for Sioux scouts unexamined. They crossed the remainder of the valley grassland, striking up into the steep, bare slopes of the divide which separated the valley of the Little Big Horn from the Rosebud valley. Up and up they climbed, their horses struggling for footholds in the dry red sandstone.

The morning was far advanced by the time they came out on the ridge, and saw the smoke of Indian cooking fires in the haze of distance far to the west.

"There they are!" said Patrick grimly.

Jim allowed his gaze to follow Patrick's pointing finger. He saw a vague blue mist hanging over the tops of a thick belt of willows and cottonwoods. Was it smoke? Or was it simply mist rising from the water of the little river? If Patrick said this was the site of the Sioux camp, then it probably was; but to Jim's untutored eyes it didn't look very convincing. He turned to look at Curly—like a doctor seeking a second opinion.

Curly was nowhere to be seen. He had disappeared in his sudden unpredictable way, hot on a fresh scent.

Jim looked back to the east, but Curley wasn't there. All that could be seen was the dust cloud which billowed up from the dry soil of the Rosebud valley as the Seventh moved steadily towards the divide. Horses and mules churned up the soil for several hundred yards as they pushed forward, the red dust all but obliterating the troopers and their officers from sight.

Jim swung his gaze, searching for Curly, but Patrick found the Crow first.

"Curley's on to somethin'!" he said suddenly. "Ride down an' see what he's found, Jim."

Jim urged his horse over the ridge, and at once saw the Indian far below, circling his pony over a wide area. He hurried down the slope to join him.

"What's up, Curly?" he asked as he drew rein beside the Crow.

"Bad Medicine," the Indian grunted. "More Sioux have ridden from the south to join their brothers, and there are plenty of Cheyennes with them." He pointed out the scars of many lodge poles in the hot dry turf— they stretched way across the valley, line after line of trailing marks and hoofprints.

"How many?" Jim asked as he regarded the never-ending tracks which all pointed from the south towards the distant trees where the smoke had been sighted.

"Too many," was all Curly said, but it was enough to send a shiver of apprehension over the bugler. "Come," the scout continued, his face set in grim lines of concentration. "We see where they camped. Then we know how many in this big village." He straightened up, looking towards the ridge where Bloody Knife sat on his horse alongside Patrick O'Keefe. With a few gestures he informed his fellow Crow where he was going and why, the next instant Jim shook his horse into a brisk trot to catch up with the Indian as he sped off across the valley.

They travelled ten miles before they came upon the first camp site. It was deserted, but there was ample evidence that the Sioux and Cheyennes had only been gone about twenty-four hours. Burned patches of grass lay in wide circles where the cooking fires had been; one circle after another, separated from each other by the marks of the lodge poles and the flattened grass where the lodges themselves had stood.

"They are ready for us," Curly said suddenly. "See. Powerful sign talk."

All Jim could see were two buffalo skulls, one bigger than the other, with a broken lance stuck in the ground between them. Around the grisly relics were man-made scratches in the soil.

"What does that mean?"

"Sioux fight talk," Curley informed him. "The bull buffalo skull is the sign for the strength and might of the Sioux. They say they will fight with the bravery of a bull. The smaller skull—that of a cow—boasts that the 'Long Knives' will run like women. The three stones in a row say that the Great Spirit has given victory to the Sioux, and if the 'Long Knives' do not attack soon they will go after them. It is bad talk. The Sioux are many, and they are confident of victory."

But Jim was only half listening to the end of Curly's unusually long speech. He was bending down reaching for something bright which glittered in the grass as the rays of the brilliant sun caught it.

"Take a look at that, Curley," he invited, straightening up with the little metal object in his hand. "There's only one gun I know uses a shell like that."

Curly regarded the brass shell for a second or two before he raised his eyes slowly to meet Jim's gaze. "The gun the white man calls a Winchester," he sighed.

" A Winchester *repeater*," Jim corrected him.

Patrick O'Keefe was worried.

The report Jim and Curly had brought back from their advanced scout was serious. Curly's estimate of the strength of the Sioux had been finalised at around fifteen hundred actual braves and fighting men—at least. Quite what the strength of the Cheyennes who rode with them was no one really knew. For all anyone could tell they might be nearly as numerous. Against that formidable force Colonel Custer had under six hundred actual fighting men and officers. The remainder of the full strength of the Seventh was comprised of bandsmen, untrained recruits, waggoners, and non-combatant troops, who had all been left behind.

Now, with Jim Peters' disturbing news that the Sioux had Winchester repeaters—the most modern weapon on the frontier—the balance of power between the forces was more than weighed in favour of Sitting Bull.

" Well, that's Custer's worry," Patrick sighed unhappily. " I've reported to the ' General ' an' now 'tis himself who has to decide what to do."

But it wasn't just Custer's worry—and in his heart of hearts Patrick O'Keefe knew that only too well. It was the concern of every man in the Seventh. Custer held their fate in the hollow of his hand. The Seventh was ahead of schedule; Terry was nowhere near in position to support them with his infantry yet. Gibbon had not crossed the Yellowstone and didn't expect to until the 26th of June. Of Crook there was still no news at all.

But General Terry's orders had left the ultimate decision to attack to Custer himself. He was to use his judgment—and to Patrick O'Keefe's way of looking at it that meant just one thing. If there was the remotest chance of a brilliant victory the " General " would welcome it, reaching out for it with both hands.

Custer was still smarting under the humiliation he had suffered in Washington. It was something that he would never forget as long as he lived. He had earned the displeasure of the President of the United States himself. He had been humbled and brought to heel like a hunting dog. He had suffered the scorn of his fellow officers of his foolishness in criticising the Government.

Only one thing could change all that, and put him back in all his former glory as the idol of the people— the dashing Cavalry commander who had risen to the heights while barely into his twenties.

That one thing was action—victory. To Custer the two words were the same. He never thought of defeat, nor even of defence. It was attack, attack, attack with him. He had done it in the Civil War, he had done it in the Battle of the Washita—and he was deuced if he wasn't going to do it now! He wasn't going to share any victory with Terry, or Gibbon, or Crook. No, sir! If there was any attacking to do and victory to be achieved it was Major-General George Armstrong Custer who was to reap the rewards and wear the victor's laurels. Share the credit with other men and other regiments? Not on your life! Not *General* Custer!

It was strange how the Seventh understood what was going through their commander's mind as he sat and brooded in his tent, just eighteen miles short of the Little Big Horn River that sultry night of June 24th, 1876. It was strange—and yet it wasn't, for those men loved their commander, for all his faults and all his bitter moods of black depression. They loved him, and they sympathised with him. His disgrace had reflected upon them personally, for he was one of them—the commander of the Seventh, *their* regiment.

They knew before he did what the decision was to be. They were fully prepared for the uproar and confusion which came as Jim Peters hurried from company commander to company commander, in the dead of night, waking the startled, bleary-eyed, snarling officers from their slumbers to give them the " General's " orders.

" Saddle and ride, sir. Colonel Custer has ordered a night march. He expects to get into position for an attack in the morning!"

" General " Custer had run true to form. He was doing the only thing possible for a man of his temperament. He was going to slam Sitting Bull hard, by surprise, and he was going to slam him once and for all, without anybody's help.

He was Custer—and he was going to attack.

CHAPTER NINETEEN

MAJOR RENO ATTACKS

THE SEVENTH struggled through the night, stumbling along the bed of a partially dried up stream, at one minute losing touch with its own companies, at other times becoming a jumbled mass of kicking horses and sweating, cursing men. But all the time it moved forwards—a regiment spoiling for a fight, driven ruthlessly forward by the personel ambition of its commander.

Dawn found the weary troopers and their sullen officers high up on a divide. They had ridden from eleven o'clock the night before. It was now 4 a.m. They fell out, thankfully, for breakfast, while Custer and Bloody Knife rode up on to a high crag and stared into the narrowing distance.

Custer was back in half an hour.

" They're dead ahead," he announced to Reno and Benteen. " I could see a few tepees through the trees of the creek, and there's smoke farther on."

"We ought to wait for Terry!" protested Reno.

Custer whirled on him. "You missed the greatest chance of your career when you failed to attack before, Major!" he thundered. "Have Boots and Saddles sounded at eight o'clock. And remember, sir, that *I* am in command!"

Reno blanched, but he held his peace. At eight o'clock Jim Peters blew his bugle for the first time on the campaign. The clear, stirring notes rang out across the empty plain, spurring the troopers out of their rest and into the creaking McClellan saddles—booted, spurred and ready.

Noon found them closing fast with the dense belt of willows which hid the Indian village from them—and protected the fast-moving troopers from observation by the Sioux.

"How d'ye feel, lad?" asked Patrick O'Keefe as he drew alongside the young bugler.

"Fine!" Jim grinned back, though his stomach was turning over and the palms of his hands were wet with sweat where they held the reins of his horse.

"That's the ticket, me bucko!" Patrick grinned back cheerfully. Secretly he was cursing Custer for a fool—worried more and more by the way the "General" was riling his second in command. "If I were Reno," he muttered to himself, "I'd feel like spittin' in Custer's face. He practically accused him o' cowardice."

They reached a ridge and Custer flung his hand high above his head in signal for a halt. They reined sharply, almost tumbling into one another. Below them a lone tepee showed white through a gap in the willows.

Bloody Knife and Curly rode forward, fast, veering away from each other as they scouted the willows. They wheeled suddenly and hurried back.

"Plenty Sioux. Many lodges!" Curly called.

Custer was exultant. "Good!" he cried, swinging in

his saddle to face his command. "You heard him, boys? There are more than enough for us all."

"Too many, too many!" Bloody Knife yelled as he too rode up. But Custer was already rapping out orders.

"They're yours, Major!" he called to Reno. "Take companies 'M,' 'G,' and 'A.' Cross the creek and attack at once. I shall support you. Take Peters as your orderly, and send him across to me if you have anything to report. Is that clear?"

Reno nodded, and Custer turned to Captain Benteen. "Benteen," he ordered, "you will hold your three companies, 'H,' 'D,' and 'K' in reserve. 'B' company will guard the ammunition train. Support us in the centre if you deem it necessary. I shall send an orderly back if I need supplies in a hurry. Understand?"

"Sir," Benteen acknowledged.

"I shall take companies 'C,' 'E,' 'F,' 'I,' and 'L'," Custer finished. "Good luck, gentlemen."

What happened next was to remain a jumbled confused memory in Jim Peters' mind. He saw Patrick O'Keefe wheel away on Custer's heels, bearing the "General's" personal guidon. He found himself closing up behind Major Reno and his lieutenants. Then all was action as the two commanders split away from the ridge at the head of their respective companies.

"Forward!" cried Reno, pointing to a gap in the willows and spurring hard towards it.

The troopers followed, tight bunched, but thinning out as they reached the water and urged their horses across in a shower of spray. Jim reached the bank and drew rein beside the major.

"Form up! Form up!" Reno was shouting as the troopers began to straggle, fighting their thirsty horses away from the water. The skirmish line took shape, and next moment Major Reno rode out at the head of his men—with the tepees of the Sioux straight ahead.

On they thundered, bending low to their horses' necks. Yelling figures darted from the lodges, grabbing up spears and bows and rifles and vaulting across the bare backs of tethered ponies. Squaws fled screaming into the dust cloud raised by their menfolk's horses. Braves appeared from all sides—painted braves, with trailing head-dresses, buckskin breech clouts and long plaited braids which danced as they moved.

"Fire into the lodges!" Reno roared, his voice almost drowned by the pounding of the horses' hooves and the shouts which were coming from all sides now.

Jim unbuttoned the flap of his holster with one hand while he clung grimly to the reins of his straining horse with the other. He drew out the heavy Colt and fired carefully, picking his target. A brave threw up his hands and fell. A second followed.

Then, suddenly, the village came into full view.

"My God!" Jim heard Reno exclaim. "There are thousands of the devils!"

It was true. The whole valley was alive with redskins. They flocked out of the shadow of the trees, from the cover of the billowing dust cloud over the horse herd, and from every nook and cranny in the broken undulating ground. The lodges filled the valley from edge to edge—a solid mass of painted buffalo hide.

A withering fire came from the massed tribesmen. Rifles spat death at the troopers, arrows whistled out of nowhere and struck at horses and riders with a frightening viciousness. Lead whined about their ears.

Jim heard the bark of a Winchester among the willows He turned in his saddle and spotted a brave steadying his rifle against a tree. He took speedy aim, fired, and the Sioux dropped like a stone.

"Dismount!"

Major Reno's stentorian shout penetrated the din of battle. Troopers reined to a halt, sprang from their saddles, throwing the reins to every third trooper, who grabbed them and hustled the horses back fifty yards.

Jim found himself beside men he had never met, firing shot after shot from his carbine as he knelt in the warm dry grass of the Little Big Horn valley and watched the Sioux come screaming towards him.

"Steady men, steady!" Reno's voice came again, and the two lieutenants repeated his words down the crescent shape of the firing line. "Steady! Make every shot tell. Don't waste your ammunition!"

The Sioux broke, wheeling away, and Jim's heart gave a jerk of relief. But it was only a temporary respite, for more and more riders appeared from the centre of the village, hurling themselves forward into battle, screaming, yelling, invoking all the spirits of the plains to aid them in their battle with the cursed Pony Soldiers of the Great White Chief in Washington.

"Bugler!"

Jim heard the cry almost in his ear. He swung around, lowering his carbine, and found Reno, hatless, flushed and perspiring like a bull, at his side.

"Ride to Custer," Reno ordered, all courtesy or rank and discipline forgotten. "Tell him I'm pulling out for the woods. We can't stand this. He *must* support me!"

"Where is he?" Jim yelled back.

"The devil only knows!" Reno answered. "Playing at soldiers on the ridge I shouldn't wonder!"

Major Reno had forgotten himself in the heat of battle. He pulled himself up sharply. "Go on, *move*!" he roared, annoyed with himself for his regrettable lapse.

Jim leapt to his feet and darted away through the smoke of exploding powder, zig-zagging as he had been taught, lest a sniper should be trying to pick him off.

There was no hope of finding his own horse. He grabbed the first one he could see, wrenching the reins from the hands of the startled horse-soldier.

He made for the river, caught sight of a party of braves slipping round behind the horse-holder, sent a shot or two winging amongst them, and veered off for the creek.

Jim didn't look back until he was across the water and heading up to the bluffs to the east, where Custer had last been seen. Then he turned, allowing his horse a brief breather, and took in the shambles he had just left.

Reno was in full retreat!

" M," " G," and " A " companies were falling back, step by step, for the woods, firing as they went. The horse-holders were fighting too as the Sioux strove to outflank them. Reno's command was in big trouble.

Higher and higher the bugler climbed, driving his horse without thought or care. Nothing mattered but to get to Custer with Reno's message before the whole attack folded up and turned into a rout.

But where was Custer?

Jim looked about wildly. He heard firing coming from the tree-lined banks further downstream. Was Custer, too, in trouble?

His horse was gasping now, pulling in great heaving lungfuls of air. But this was no time to consider his mount; the lives of the three companies depended upon him getting to Custer. Ruthlessly he dug his spurs in and lashed the horse forward with the trailing end of his reins.

Custer had an eye for country and short cuts which was second to none. Without pausing for a second he selected his route to the north end of the Sioux village and swung his five companies up to the bluffs. Beyond, if his judgment was sound, they were sure to find a ravine cutting the hillsides and leading straight down to the shallow ford on the Little Big Horn which he had selected as his point of attack. They would be able to approach at speed, unseen, and slam the Sioux where they were least expecting it.

Custer was right. He reached the top of the bluff, with Lt. Cooke and Patrick O'Keefe close behind him, and saw at once that the ravine lay just where he had expected it.

"There goes Reno!" called Cooke, pointing to the charging troopers of "M," "G," and "A" companies, strung out along the valley on the far side of the river.

Custer nodded, his professional eye noting and approving the way his second in command had formed up his men and kept them together.

"Just like the old days, eh, Sergeant?" the commander grinned at Patrick O'Keefe.

But Patrick was staring off at the massed tepees showing vaguely through the trees, all along the banks of the river for as far as the eye could see. "Take a look down there, sorr!" he said quietly. "There's no end to the lodges!"

Custer whirled, his face hardening as he saw the extent of the Indian village.

"It's going to be quite a fight," he said grimly. He turned to his adjutant. "Send Bugler Martin back to Benteen. Tell him to hurry forward and bring the ammunition packs. We're going to need them."

First Lieutenant Cooke scribbled hastily in his field note-book, ripped off the page and handed it to the waiting orderly who had ridden forward from the ranks of the grey-horsed "E" company.

"Take this to Captain Benteen—and hurry!" he rapped out.

Martin wheeled away.

The message he carried read. *Benteen. Come on. Big Village. Be Quick. Bring Packs.* Signed, *W. W. Cooke.*

It was the only written order of the whole battle. It

was to take its place in the archives of the United States Army.

"We must attack farther downstream," Custer was saying. "We're only in the middle of the village. We must find a way to approach from the end and pin the Sioux between Reno's force and our own."

"Can Reno hold them until we're in position?" Cooke asked.

"He's got to!" Custer roared as he urged his horse forward to cross the ravine. "The whole battle depends upon him."

Patrick O'Keefe was more than worried now. He was experiencing what the Confederate forces had felt at Gettysburg, and what Napoleon's troops had felt at Waterloo. He was scenting the air of battle—and smelling danger, and the premonition of defeat.

"It all depends upon Reno," he thought as he rode forward down the slope clutching the "General's" personal guidon. "And he's the weakest link in the chain. He has failed once already. He'll pull out, as sure as eggs are eggs, if he thinks the odds are too great."

At that moment, Major Marcus Reno was realising he had bitten off more than he could chew—thanks to Custer's refusal to wait for General Terry. He was shouting for Jim Peters. He was demanding support that Custer was unable to give. He was the weak link —and he was already breaking.

CHAPTER TWENTY

CUSTER'S LAST STAND

IT WAS the Cheyennes who sealed the fate of the Seventh. Under the skilled, fast-thinking leadership of their war chief, they had sped through the main village of the Sioux from their camp at the north end of the valley, to aid Crazy Horse, Gall and Sitting Bull in their defence of the village against Reno's troopers. It was *their* dust Reno had seen as the first wave of Sioux broke under his volleys, and it was their braves who had spread out behind the horse-holders to cut off his retreat.

They were cousins of the Sioux—close cousins, related by blood and intermarriage. They were the famous "Dog Soldiers" of the plains—as experienced in war as Custer himself, and just as brave.

The Sioux waited for an attack to develop and fought as individuals protecting their village by weight of numbers and with no prearranged plan of action.

The Cheyennes fought as a team, their war chiefs using their heads as well as their might.

The minute Two Moon and White Bull saw that the succeeding waves of Sioux warriors were well able to cope with Reno's men, they sped through their circling braves, pointing back to the village. It was time to worry about their own camp. The White Eyes had a nasty habit of striking in two places at once, and they were taking no chances.

"Back! Back, O my warriors!" White Bull screamed high above the din of battle.

"To your lodges!" Two Moon took up the cry, rearing his war-horse high as he flourished his coup stick. "Leave these carrion to our cousins, the mighty Sioux, lest Yellowhair strikes from behind us!"

The Cheyennes heard their chiefs, and hesitated. They were mad with blood-lust, chanting their death songs as they wheeled and circled, urging each other on to further deeds of bravery in the face of the lead that sang up at them from the Colts and Springfields.

They heard—and many of them chose to ignore their leaders. They were not to be robbed so easily of the white men's scalps that were their rightful trophies. They shook their ungainly, long-tailed mustangs into a gallop, straight for the portion of the wavering line of blue-coated troopers which was the thinnest. On and on they rode, weaving this way and that, as did their Sioux cousins, heads low and war shields high.

"Hoka Hey!" they cried. "Hoka Hey! Death to the white dogs!"

But there were others among the weaving, darting, circling horsemen who heeded their war-chiefs. They thought, in the fleeting second of their hesitation, of the squaws and young children they had left behind in their Cheyenne camp site when they sprang to the aid of the Sioux. They heard their chiefs, and knew their words were wise. These were warriors of experience. These were the élite—the "Dog Soldiers" of the Cheyenne tribe.

Leaving their hot-headed younger brothers to drive the troopers farther and farther back to the woods and the river beyond, they hauled their ponies round, jerking their leathery mouths with characteristic savagery and disregard for horseflesh. They turned and raced back through the village, clearing cooking fires in a single leap, twisting in and out among the tepees, scattering the startled Sioux who still flocked to the attack.

"Make way, O my cousins!" Two Moon yelled as he cut through to where Sitting Bull and Chief Gall of the Uncpapa Sioux sat on their gaily-decked horses and watched the progress of the battle they had awaited for long, patient months. "We ride to protect our lodges from the Pony Soldiers of Yellowhair!"

Sitting Bull nodded gravely. "You have done well, cousin, and you are wise. I wish I could ride with you, but my place is here among my people."

Chief Gall flung up his hand. "Yonder rides Crazy Horse!" he called. "Take him and his Ogallala warriors with you, Two Moon. It is good that the Sioux and the Cheyenne should fight together."

"Save Yellowhair for me!" Sitting Bull called as the Cheyennes sped away down the crowded valley. "I have waited long for that one's scalp!"

"Hurry—or you will be too late!"

Two Moon's cackling cry came back to the Sioux Medicine Man through the swirling dust of the Little Big Horn valley.

Coming out of the second ravine above the river shallows, Colonel Custer saw the dust rising high above the tree-tops. He saw it—and misread its meaning.

"By Golly! Reno's got them on the run!" he cried. "We're just in time!" He flashed his sabre from its scabbard and flung it high. "Forward!" he yelled in a voice that echoed up the coulee from rock to rock above the heads of the tight-packed troopers of his five companies. "Forward to the river!"

"E" company jerked into motion, their matched grey horses prancing and clattering over the rocky ground to the jingle of spurs and the slap of carbine slings. "C" company moved forward, "F" followed, and "L" swung into action hard on their tails.

"This is it, Sergeant," Captain Miles Keogh grinned to Schultz, who rode beside him at the head of "I" company, in the rearguard. "Now's your chance to earn a Congressional Medal to go with those other ribbons."

First Sergeant Schultz grunted. "I'm too busy prayin', sir," he cracked back.

"Me too," muttered Trooper Larkin to Trooper Siggers—but *he* wasn't joking. He had the same premonition of disaster that had settled like a black cloud over Patrick O'Keefe.

Custer rode at full tilt for the wide, gravel bar of the

ford, with the companies fanning out behind him over the noon-dry grass.

Glancing at the commander, Patrick O'Keefe saw his head lift, and his buckskin-clad shoulders square. He caught the expression on the "General's" face and read it for what it was—a look of triumph. This was to be his greatest hour. The moment when the Sioux were beginning to break, and he, Custer, was to deal the final crushing blow! He could all but taste the sweet nectar of victory.

And then they saw them.

The Cheyennes and the Sioux burst out of the dust cloud and through the trees like a whirlwind. They hurled themselves for the river bank with a concerted howl that turned every soldier's blood cold with fear.

In that instant Jim Peters arrived at the head of the coulee. He was in time to see Custer leap from his horse as an arrow from Crazy Horse's bow flew straight to its heart. He heard the bark of rifles and the curt, rasping commands as the troopers scattered, backing away from that water that was thick with Indians. Carbines lifted, spitting lead into the packed horde of Cheyennes and Sioux, covering their colonel as he staggered to his feet, dazed and unbelieving.

Jim saw Patrick O'Keefe lean sideways in his saddle, the Indians forgotten as he seized his commander's hand and hauled him up on to the back of his horse, before wheeling away from the water. In that moment Jim knew that Custer's command was doomed.

Slowly, bitterly, Colonel Custer and his troops fell back from the water, fighting every inch of the way.

Mounted on the horse of a fallen trooper, Custer was everywhere, cheering his men by his own example, aiding the wounded, and keeping the firmest grip on the situation that it was in his power to do. He fought the action of his life—an ordered retreat to the bluffs by the 225 men at his command, in the face of 2,000 howling, well-armed Indians.

Jim Peters saw it all as he waited at the head of the coulee for the first mad confusion to die down. Then, as the Indians reached the bank and began to scatter for cover, he jerked his horse into action and dashed out of the coulee, across the slope, and into the battle, with the report from Reno which was now utterly valueless.

Custer heard him out in silence as he shouted to make himself heard above the terrifying din. When he had finished the Colonel shrugged and spread his hands wide. There was no need for words. There was nothing he could do. The troops who should have supported Reno were now fighting for their very lives.

"Take your place with your company, lad," was all the Colonel could say. "We need every able-bodied man we can raise."

And then some of the old fire returned to the commander of the Seventh Cavalry. "My compliments to Captain Keogh. Ask him to dismount his company and cover a counter attack!" he roared.

Jim didn't need any urging. He raced forward, dodging the bullets and arrows that were coming in from all directions now. He came to a slithering halt beside his old company commander and passed on the message.

"A counter attack! By hokey that man's got guts!"

A brief, crooked smile lifted the corners of Captain Keogh's mouth, and then he was shouting to his men to dismount, and take cover behind rocks or sage brush, or whatever they could find. "Here, catch!" he called to Jim, and Comanche's reins sailed through the air towards him. "If anything happens to me, Peters, Comanche is yours."

Jim was about to stammer his thanks when Sergeant Schultz broke in with a warning cry. "Look down there, sir!" he called. "There are hundreds more Injuns comin' to join the first lot! It'd be suicide for the Colonel to attack now."

Captain Keogh's face was lined with strain. He nodded briefly. "Peters," he ordered, putting his mouth to Jim's ear to make himself heard. "Tell the Colonel what we've seen. Tell him I will hold this position with the aid of Lieutenant Calhoun and "L" company for as long as I can. Then I will retire to the crown of the bluff where he is."

"Yessir." Jim stepped up into Comanche's saddle and was away.

Before he was halfway across the slope Captain Keogh was dead, and ten men of his company with him. All hope of a counter-attack had faded, and the troopers were already falling back to the brow of the bluff.

Other companies were in trouble too. Man after man was dropping to the accurate fire of the Indians, who had dismounted now and were wriggling their way up through the brush and the draws and coulees of the broken country all around. Twenty horses had stampeded, many others were dead or dying—"C" and "E" companies had used the carcasses of their horses to build a breastwork round the crown of the bluff where Custer directed the battle. First Lieutenant Cooke was mortally wounded, Captain Yates was dead, Custer was wounded in the shoulder—and ammunition was running low.

"Where in tarnation has Benteen got to?" Custer was complaining as Jim appeared.

It was Patrick O'Keefe who answered. It was the first Jim had seen of the sergeant since the attack began. He was dismounted, crouched behind the body of his horse with a Springfield nestled firmly in his shoulder. "Dug in with the remains o' Major Reno's command —if he's got any sense," he shouted. "He's got no chance o' gettin' through to us now, Colonel."

It was true, and Custer knew it. From the bursts of firing that were coming to them from the distance it was plain that Reno had fallen back across the river and was entrenched, surrounded and pinned down by Sitting Bull's warriors. All hope of relief had evaporated in the heat of battle—just when it was needed most. Benteen would be able to get no further than Reno's position. More and more Sioux and Cheyennes were streaming across the river now, switching their attentions from the shattered remnant of Reno's companies to the larger force that still remained with Custer. Lying there on the bluff they saw Gall and Sitting Bull ride out across the ford with a seemingly endless stream of braves splashing their way through the sluggish water behind them.

Sitting Bull was moving in for the kill. He had come to claim the scalp of Yellowhair.

Custer was crouched beside Jim and Patrick, grey-faced with pain, a haunted look in his eyes. There were barely forty men left now of the two hundred he had led down to the river. The sun was burning down with relentless heat, drying their tongues, fetching out the streaming perspiration with every move of their bodies.

A hail of arrows and a few scattered shots came from the left flank.

"They're getting round behind us!" Lieutenant Smith of "E" company yelled, leaping to his feet and blazing away at the darting figures who were making for the rear of the bluff. A dozen bullets caught him, spinning him around. He dropped at Jim's feet—the last survivor of his company.

Jim was petrified with fear now. He was looking Death full in the face and he was dreading what he saw. His mind flashed back to the Black Hills, to the gold he and Uncle Moses and Patrick had discovered and mined, and which was now valueless.

That gold had been the start of it all.

It had touched off the greed that lay deep within them all. It had caused the frontiersmen to break their word and their treaty. It had caused the death of his uncle and many other ordinary folk. It had driven the Sioux to make one last break for freedom. Its discovery had brought the Seventh to this bare, ugly bluff to be shattered and destroyed by the vengeful might of Sitting Bull and his Cheyenne cousins. It had been the beginning of the end.

A sudden gasp beside him brought Jim back to reality. Patrick O'Keefe was coughing, choking. A tell-tale splodge of red was oozing across his shirt.

"Patrick!" Jim screamed. "Patrick! Oh no!"

Sergeant Patrick O'Keefe tried to smile, but his lips barely moved.

"I'm done for, lad," he gasped. "The gold is yours now. Do what ye will with it." He choked once more and crumpled, Custer's personal guidon still fluttering bravely beside him in the afternoon breeze.

Custer moved across, wincing at the pain from his wound.

"O'Keefe," he called, but there was no answer. He turned the sergeant over, then let him fall back beside his overheated Springfield.

Patrick O'Keefe was dead.

Lieutenant-Colonel Custer looked into the eyes of the seventeen-year-old bugler he had taken as his personal orderly. He saw the tears of anguish, fear and loneliness that were welling up in the boy's eyes, and read the horror written clear on his powder-blackened face.

It was then that the man who had been a major-general remembered his duty—saw where he had failed. He had brought death and destruction to the Seventh by his personal greed for glory. He had forgotten that a commander was only as strong as the team behind him.

George Armstrong Custer remembered now the other

members of his team, his regiment. "Peters. Peters. Find Reno. Cut loose and find Reno," he croaked. "There's just a chance that a lone horseman will get through. Find Reno and tell him not to attempt a counter attack. Tell him to conserve his men to fight another day. The Seventh isn't finished yet." He reached for his cavalry sabre. "Here," he ordered. "Take my sabre and use it well. There's just a chance, if you have the will, and the courage."

As in a dream, or a horrible nightmare, Jim took the sabre, feeling the firm, worn strength of the polished hilt. He looked wildly around him at the pitiful remnant of five full companies of cavalry. He heard Comanche neigh high with fear as an arrow grazed his flank.

And then he was leaping up into the saddle of the finest horse he had ever ridden. He felt Comanche lurch forward, and tear down the rear slope, straight for the Sioux who sought to close the last fifty yards of gaunt, brush-clad hillside.

He turned once in the saddle before he was among the Indians. He saw Custer standing, bravely, proudly, before his guidon and the flag of America, facing the oncoming hordes of Sioux who rode in for the kill.

Lieutenant-Colonel Custer of the Seventh was making his last stand in the only way he knew how—bravely and spectacularly.

Jim turned away, his eyes blurred with tears of shock and misery. He saw the Sioux flinging themselves towards him. He raked Comanche's sides with his spurs, calling to the bay for one last effort of speed. He fired his revolver, left-handed, into the faces of the braves, shooting wildly, without care or thought, pulling and pulling the trigger of the Colt until its hammer clicked and clicked again, harmlessly on empty chambers.

And then he was among them, and nearly through them, slashing, cutting, thrusting with Custer's sabre—

fighting for his very life. Comanche screamed with pain, staggered once, then again, but picked up his stride and opened out with all he had got—an arrow in his flank, another in the fleshy part of his neck.

Another crazy mix-up of flaying hooves and jumbled, floundering pain-streaked bodies, and they were through the Sioux and speeding for the rising land beyond.

The crack of exploding cartridges sounded behind them. Arrows plucked at Jim's clothes, sliced Comanche's hide, and bullets sang their death song about their ears—but they were through. Moving faster than the wind itself over the sagebrush slopes.

Quite how far they rode Jim never knew. He was in a daze, his mind centred on one thing and one thing only—to get to Reno with the " General's " last message.

He came to his senses with the pain of his stiffening wounds. He hadn't even known that he had been hit until then. Comanche too was faltering, wounded in seven places, but still gamely pounding on.

Jim reined to a halt and looked back.

It was all over. The Sioux had over-run the bluff. They were everywhere packed in one whirling, wheeling, exultant mob, snatching up trophies, chanting their victory songs.

Yellowhair and his men had fallen. The battle was over.

Slowly Jim reached with fumbling hands for the bugle that still hung about his neck. Gingerly, wincing at the pain from his wounds, he put it to his lips.

Softly, then louder and louder as a new strength surged through him, the mournful, lonely call of " Taps " rose up from the barren bluff, echoing among the ravines and coulees and fading into the distance that was the valley of the Little Big Horn River. It was four o'clock on the afternoon of Sunday, 25th of June, 1876.

It wasn't until the 26th that Jim Peters was able to

get through to Major Reno and Captain Benteen in their entrenchments on a southern hillside where they nursed their wounded and regrouped their few fighting men to search for the main body of the Seventh.

The battle of the Little Big Horn was over. The Sioux had moved on to celebrate their victory, and Major Marcus Reno learned then that Jim Peters and Comanche were the sole survivors of five full companies of " General " Custer's Fighting Seventh.

THE END